I0825292

# The SOMEWHAT WICKED WITCH of BRIGANDALE

## TITLES BY C. M. WAGGONER

*Unnatural Magic*
*The Ruthless Lady's Guide to Wizardry*
*The Village Library Demon-Hunting Society*

*The Somewhat Wicked Witch of Brigandale*

# *The* SOMEWHAT WICKED WITCH *of* BRIGANDALE

C. M. WAGGONER

ACE
*New York*

ACE
Published by Berkley
An imprint of Penguin Random House LLC
1745 Broadway, New York, NY 10019
penguinrandomhouse.com

Book design by Daniel Brount

Library of Congress Cataloging-in-Publication Data

Names: Waggoner, C. M., author.
Title: The somewhat wicked witch of Brigandale / C.M. Waggoner.
Description: New York: Ace, 2026.
Identifiers: LCCN 2025029627 (print) | LCCN 2025029628 (ebook) |
ISBN 9798217188239 hardcover | ISBN 9798217188246 ebook
Subjects: LCGFT: Fantasy fiction | Novels
Classification: LCC PS3623.A3533 S66 2026 (print) |
LCC PS3623.A3533 (ebook)
LC record available at https://lccn.loc.gov/2025029627
LC ebook record available at https://lccn.loc.gov/2025029628

Printed in the United States of America
1st Printing

The authorized representative in the EU for product safety and compliance is Penguin Random House Ireland, Morrison Chambers, 32 Nassau Street, Dublin D02 YH68, Ireland, https://eu-contact.penguin.ie.

*For my dad: my first reading and writing role model, enthusiastic unpaid publicist, and favorite defender of democracy. I'm still looking forward to reading your memoirs.*

# The SOMEWHAT WICKED WITCH of BRIGANDALE

CHAPTER 1

# In Which Gretsella Receives an Unusual Delivery

Once upon a time, on a somewhat muggy Wednesday afternoon in late August, the witch Gretsella arrived home to her cottage in the Dark Forest of Brigandale in the Kingdom of Evermore to find a bottle of milk on her steps. There was also a screaming baby.

The milk was there because the milkman always came on Wednesdays. Gretsella paid him to do so. She didn't know when or why a babyman had come as well, though it seemed clear that when the babyman cameth, he had cometh for her. Attached to the baby's ankle was a luggage tag that read "To be taken into the care of Gretsella, the Witch of Brigandale with the Reasonable Prices." This was, in fact, Gretsella's preferred epithet. When it came to making a career out of witchery in today's economy, whether you were a *good* witch or a *bad* witch was of less concern than whether you were a witch whose subtle arts were accessible to the middle-class homemaker.

The baby was still screaming.

"Stop that," Gretsella said.

The baby did.

"Well, at least you know your manners," Gretsella said, and carried the baby inside.

Gretsella's cottage was a nice, cozy little place, if Gretsella said so herself, which Gretsella often did. Gretsella was firmly convinced that her home could not be surpassed by the finest mansions in all of Evermore. On this point, she might not have been entirely incorrect. It was a cottage perfectly positioned and enchanted to catch only the coolest, most fragrant breezes in summer, and in winter it was always snug and warm and smelled of the rosemary tincture that Gretsella used for everything from washing her hair to mixing up a fortifying drink with a modest slug of gin. There were always fresh sweet rushes on the floor, and the hearth was swept as clean as the dinner plates. It was, in short, a very wholesome atmosphere for a baby to visit, if a baby saw fit to go visiting. Gretsella could think of no reason why the baby shouldn't be invited inside.

Though she had never had any children of her own, Gretsella had never found herself particularly intimidated by babies. As she saw it, they were a bit like wolves and termites and fast-growing asymmetrical moles: One only needed to be *firm* with them. That was, at least, her own experience. She'd noticed that people who had the misfortune *not* to be witches seemed to find things a bit more difficult. In any case, within half an hour or so, she had given the baby a thorough scrubbing down in a dishpan and diapered him with a clean tea towel, then set him down in a breadbasket, where he proceeded to placidly gnaw upon his own fist.

"I don't see why *you're* looking so satisfied with yourself," Gretsella said. "A helpless infant all alone in the world, with no way to make an honest living."

The baby had nothing to say for himself.

"And why give me a baby?" Gretsella asked him. "It isn't as if I took out an advertisement in the paper. *Wanted: one able infant-of-all-work.* Ridiculous! Of what possible use could you be?"

The baby made no reply.

"Ah, well, if you *insist* on being difficult, I suppose there isn't anything else for it," Gretsella said, and began to search the cottage for supplies to make the baby a more comfortable bed.

Over the next few days, Gretsella and the baby embarked upon their new life together, and she found herself growing fond of him. It was a bit like having a particularly useless familiar. Her last familiar had been a black cat who could smell demons. The baby mostly smelled terrible. He was lovable, though, in his own way. Gretsella had worked miracles for people who expressed less joy and enthusiasm for her efforts than the baby did whenever she pretended that a spoonful of mashed peas was an owl flying into the hollow of a tree.

She decided to name him Bradley.

Bradley was, on the whole, a very well-behaved young person. He only very rarely made a fuss in the evenings. On these occasions, Gretsella would sing him to sleep with songs of her own invention, which tended to run along broadly similar lines:

*Go to sleep, little baby, and don't give me cause*
*To feed you to creatures with sharp shiny claws.*
*The forest is teeming with creatures who creep,*
*So quit with your crying and go straight to sleep!*

This generally seemed to do the trick.

ONE DAY—AFTER BRADLEY HAD BEEN SLEEPING IN ONE OF her bureau drawers and dirtying her tea towels for almost a week—Gretsella was outside hanging some laundry on the line, with Bradley grubbing around in the grass by her feet, when she heard horses approaching.

She straightened up and glared in the direction of the sound as two armored men came riding into sight. "You there! Old woman!" one of them called out.

She glared harder. "*Witch.*"

"You!" the soldier said.

"Yes, *me*," she said. "I'm a *witch*. Now try that again."

"Oh," the soldier said. "You there! Witch!"

"Yes?" Gretsella said politely.

The soldier took a moment to sit up taller in his saddle

before he got to the point. "Have you seen any strange babies around here?"

Gretsella frowned. "Why do you ask?"

"Oh," the soldier said, with a glance at his companion, "no reason."

This didn't strike Gretsella as particularly convincing. "No," she said after a moment. "There aren't any strange babies here."

"But what about that one?" the second soldier asked, and pointed at Bradley, who was stuffing a fistful of grass into his mouth.

"He's not strange; he's *Bradley*," Gretsella said. "He's *my* baby."

The soldier looked somewhat dubious. "He doesn't *look* much like you."

This was, in fairness, quite true. Gretsella was very tall and very thin and very pale, with green eyes and freckles and a long, crooked nose and an unmanageable head of graying red curls. Bradley, being a mere infant, was very short and very fat. He also had a tuft of straight black hair growing out of the center of his forehead, a complexion a shade or two darker than Gretsella's own, and merry dark eyes, which were nearly swallowed up by what persons more sentimental than Gretsella might deem *irresistibly* chubby little cheeks. Gretsella drew herself up a bit. "Bradley," she said, "has no obligation whatsoever to look like anyone but himself."

The soldiers seemed unable to mount any objections to

this argument. The first soldier cleared his throat. "And aren't you a bit long in the tooth to have a child of that age?"

Gretsella's glare intensified. "I have no obligation whatsoever to be of any age other than my own," she said. "Now go away, both of you. *Shoo.*"

The soldiers stayed where they were. Gretsella turned her attention to their horses and gave each of them a good long look straight in the eye. Then she said, very firmly, "*Go away*, and *don't come back.*"

The horses left. The soldiers, being mounted on their backs, left with them. Gretsella finished hanging out her laundry, and then she and Bradley set up a nice old-fashioned soldier-, salesman-, taxman-, and missionary-repelling perimeter around the garden. "I don't know why it's been so long since I set one of these up," Gretsella said to Bradley. "What a negligent witch Mother is! Isn't that *right*, Bradley?"

Bradley cooed.

# A Digression on the Subject of Witches

Once upon a time, a long time ago, a lonely little girl wandered through a dark wood. The little girl had a real name, but everybody called her Carrots. She climbed up onto a low branch in a tree—she was the sort of little girl who would climb as high as there were convenient handholds, but no higher—made herself comfortable, and thought about the universe. She didn't stumble upon any remarkable insights. She was an ordinary little girl, not a philosopher-king.

Despite this, the universe said, *Hmm.*

If you're the sort of person who reads, you'll be aware that fairy tales ought to be taken seriously in their essence, if not in their particularity. Fairy tales, like fairies themselves, are not overly concerned with factual accuracy. They sometimes mislead. You should, therefore, take the following explanation of a peculiar phenomenon with a grain of salt: It's a little-known fact that, in the Kingdom of Evermore, just as caterpillars turn into butterflies, lonely little girls sometimes turn into witches.

The loneliness that creates a witch can't be the temporary loneliness of a child whose parents have left her alone to fend for herself for an afternoon. It's a deeper and more abiding loneliness than that. It's the sort of loneliness felt by a little girl who, for whatever reason, walks alone into the woods and climbs up into trees to think about the universe more often than she's invited to birthday parties. It's the sort of loneliness that, over time, curdles into something that isn't loneliness at all. This was the way in which Carrots was lonely.

Carrots was eleven years old. She wasn't an orphan and didn't have a cruel stepmother, and she wasn't bullied by the other children for some distinct physical attribute. She was simply a little girl who was slightly too plain, slightly too loud, and slightly too intense in her contemplation of peculiar subjects. She wasn't a round peg being forced into a square hole. She was, in a world of round holes, a peg that at some point in the manufacturing process had been made very slightly oblong, to the degree that the cosmic carpenter assumed that he was probably just hammering wrong and set her aside to try again later. This was always a particular source of pain for Carrots. If she were bullied for being the lone child with flashing green eyes and flame-colored hair in a village of dull, ordinary-looking children, that would be one thing. She'd be able to anticipate going on an exciting hero's journey and meeting lots of people who would recognize her remarkable qualities for what they were. Carrots, unfortunately, was shunned by the other children not because they were nasty provincial little bullies but because she was the sort of child who read a lot of books, thought she understood more about the world than she actually did, and didn't understand how to play with the other children without annoying them. This made her very lonely, but she told herself that she didn't care about those dull, silly children in the village anyway.

All of this was made worse by the fact that the pain felt by a lonely little girl is taken seriously by almost nobody, including the little girl herself. She is forced, therefore, to imagine herself into a world where she is a more important and interesting person experiencing a more important and interesting kind of pain. It is this specific combination of loneliness, pain, and inward-directed imaginative power that creates the ideal alluvium for germinating the seeds of witchcraft.

This condition of proto-witchery is not, strictly speaking, limited to little girls, though they experience it more frequently than any other type of person. Just as, under the right circumstances, towering trees can be found growing inside dark caves or clinging to the sides of sheer rock faces, this type of little-girl loneliness sometimes finds its expression in an embittered young widow, a forlorn and delicate elderly man, or, in one notable case, a desperately unhappy forty-five-year-old sergeant major struggling to reacclimate to civilian life after many years of fighting overseas. It is, however, an absolute fact that unhappy little girls are the ideal existential ceramic crock for fermenting the supernatural sauerkraut that is a fully developed adult witch.

Despite this rich, dark loam of little-girl loneliness being endemic in girls between the ages of seven and seventeen, it is not *sufficient* for a girl to become a witch. It's generally more likely to produce an adult with a slightly above-average level of interest in stories about notorious and gruesome murders. Even in the intensely magical forest of Brigandale, all that this sort of loneliness creates is a small divot in the fabric of reality. Most lonely little girls are too busy *living* in reality to notice a crack in it.

That day in the tree, Carrots looked at reality, noticed a handhold in it, and pulled herself up.

CHAPTER 1.5

# A Return to the Narrative That Was Interrupted by the Preceding Digression

After Bradley had been living with her for a month or so, Gretsella decided that there was no use in putting off the inevitable any longer. It was, in witch circles, generally considered perfectly respectable to raise a child who had been abandoned on one's doorstep, but one did have to observe the usual customs. Gretsella made coffee and cake and set out an extra umbrella stand to accommodate the broomsticks. She went to her front door and, on the sign that hung there, moved the arrow pointer from NOT AT HOME: GO AWAY to RECEIVING COVEN: GO AWAY. Then she waited.

Hyssop and Yarrow were the first to arrive, riding two to a broomstick, as usual. Their matching names and stout figures often led people to the mistaken impression that they were related in some way. The truth of the matter was that they were, in fact, longtime business partners, and had selected their botanical witchnames in order to better promote themselves as the type of old-fashioned, rosy-cheeked village herbalists whom one could really trust to make a healing salve or efficacious philter without any rat poison in it. They had become so successful at their venture that they'd opened an apothecary in the capital, bought themselves a large town house apiece, and had not so much as harvested a sprig of lavender for a scented sachet with their own hands in almost ten years. Their abandonment of traditional witchly occupations in favor of success in the world of commerce had opened them up to a certain degree of criticism from their fellow witches. Gretsella, for her part, put much of the criticism down to jealousy over the fact that the complainers hadn't concocted the scheme themselves.

The next to land in the garden was Magnetia, a very young witch who was ceaselessly torn between her desire to be taken seriously by her elders and her alarming propensity for doing things like buying a metal whisk with gears and a crank on it for mixing her potions. She arrived wearing all black, despite a summer heat that would convince even the most tradition-bound old crone to assent to some navy blue, and riding a broomstick that had been outfitted with what appeared to be a rubber pad for sitting on.

Then, at last, came the final member of their coven. She arrived late, as always. Barb (she claimed to have selected this peculiar witchname after having spent several days in dread communion with a spirit from a dark realm known as Weehawken) was married (to a *man*, of all things) and had given birth to several (it seemed rude to inquire as to the exact number) children, who often prevented her from leaving her house in a timely fashion for, presumably, their own iniquitous purposes (Gretsella preferred not to dwell too much on the details of what might occur within such an unnatural household). Barb lived just off the main street in a very ordinary village, where, it was rumored, she sometimes crossed hallowed ground in order to participate in a profane ritual she called "the annual church spaghetti dinner."

Gretsella, who abhorred all gossip except when she was the one maliciously spreading it, could certainly not say whether or not these rumors might be true, and had made herself a bit of an object of controversy among local witches by inviting Barb to join her coven in the first place. Despite her eccentricities, though, Barb was a valued coven member and a hag after Gretsella's own heart: Her accomplishments as an enchantress were undeniable, and even when Gretsella called for a witches' convocation on very short notice, Barb could be relied on to bring a dessert.

Today, in honor of Bradley's naming day, she had brought a crumb cake.

The witches all gathered in Gretsella's sitting room for coffee, cake, and the admiring of Bradley. Dressed in one of the little suits Gretsella had finally, begrudgingly, knitted for him, he was passed from hand to hand, and complimentary remarks were paid to his person.

"He looks awfully young for you to have lured him here, Gretsella," said Magnetia, who was not very well acquainted with small children.

Hyssop and Yarrow cackled like the respectable hags they were. Barb, like the notorious iconoclast *she* was, explained: "Bradley wasn't *lured*, Maggie. He was *abandoned*. It's very traditional to leave a lost prince on the doorstep of a local witch. Was it a loyal nurse who left him, Gretsella?"

Gretsella blinked. Much as it would have embarrassed her to admit it, if Gretsella were capable of embarrassment, she'd been too occupied with tending to Bradley to spend much time thinking about who must have brought him to her, or why. "I don't know," she said. "I suppose it might have been. Have any princes gone missing in the past month or so?"

"You haven't *heard*?" Magnetia asked, in great apparent shock. "It's been in all of the papers! The dear queen died just after the birth of her first and only child, King Weltham was fatally thrown from his horse, and the poor little prince was stolen from his cradle in the night! King Weltham's uncle Horack will be crowned king in only a week!"

"I don't read *papers*," Gretsella said witheringly. "I'm a *witch*." If there was anything she needed to know, she would scry it herself; she didn't need to *read papers*. She looked down at Bradley. "So Bradley is the infant son?"

"He *might* be," Magnetia said.

"Almost certainly," Yarrow said.

"Well," Gretsella said after a moment, "shall we have our naming celebration?"

There are, it must be admitted, very few distinct differences between a witch's naming celebration and what might otherwise be referred to as a *christening*. The difference is the *intent*, and their intent was devoid of all concepts of sin or salvation and very full of frogspawn and cackling. They cackled their way through the traditional phrases for the benefit of a deeply unaffected-looking Bradley. Then it was time for the gift giving.

Hyssop and Yarrow stepped forward first. "To you, Bradley," Hyssop said, "we grant the gift of beauty."

Gretsella was unsurprised. It was, after all, a very traditional gift to grant to a possibly royal baby, and Hyssop and Yarrow were, in their own ways, staunch traditionalists. Magnetia was frowning. "Shouldn't it be *handsomeness*, for a boy baby?"

"Oh, *really*," Yarrow said. "If beauty is good enough for a woman, then it's certainly good enough for a *man*." Yarrow was of the school of witchery that detested men.

Magnetia immediately conceded the point—she was too intent upon becoming a hag in good standing among her peers to argue with a bit of stuffy old-fashioned misandry—and then stepped forward to grant her own gift. "To you, Bradley," she said, "I grant the gift of politeness." Then, a bit too loudly: "It's very important for *children* to know how to be polite." Magnetia made occasional attempts to ally herself with the school of witchery that detested children.

Yarrow and Hyssop murmured approvingly. Then Barb stepped forward. Everyone else watched with a degree of apprehension. It was always nerve-racking when a witch so disconcertingly fixated on *originality* was allowed to bless a baby.

"To you, Bradley," Barb said, "I grant the gift of a powerful right hook."

The assembled crones all gasped. "Barb!" Hyssop said. "Do you really think it wise to grant a baby such a violent gift? What if he grows up to be a *husband*?" Hyssop knew nothing at all about husbands except for the things she'd heard from women who had come to her seeking help in eliminating their own.

Barb appeared unruffled. "Well," she said, "I'm sure Gretsella would never raise a child who would hurt someone else unprovoked, but that doesn't keep other people from bothering *him*. If Bradley is beautiful, no one will want to bother him. And if he's polite, then he should be able to talk his way out of any trouble. But if he ever *does* get into trouble, then a powerful right hook certainly won't hurt."

Gretsella imagined someone threatening Bradley with violence. Bradley, in his breadbasket, burbled and pulled off his own sock. Were he denied the gift of a powerful right hook, Gretsella wasn't sure that she liked his prospects in a brawl. "So may it be!" she declared, and Bradley was well and truly named, and ready to embark upon what Gretsella hoped would be an utterly unremarkable life.

CHAPTER 2

# In Which Gretsella Is Continuously Aggravated by Prophecy

Over the next few years, Bradley grew up, which Gretsella refused to find impressive. It didn't, after all, take any sort of extraordinary ability for a baby to grow larger. They did it without any effort whatsoever. There was nothing at all to applaud about a baby growing up into a sturdy little boy, or that little boy growing up into a tall and handsome and *excessively* likable young man.

Even Gretsella had to admit that Bradley was *bafflingly* likable. She prided herself on rarely tolerating anyone, but she was *extremely* tolerant of Bradley. It wasn't the thick black hair or the gleaming white teeth or the winsome dimple in his chin that did it. Generally, Gretsella was staunchly unmoved by the winsome dimples of the menfolk. It also wasn't his excellence at all of the sports the boys played in the village, or his pleasant baritone singing voice, or his talent for dancing.

Bradley was likable not because he was good-looking and talented but because he was constantly, effortlessly *kind.* He was the sort of young man who would dance with the plainest girl at the wedding so that she didn't feel left out. He was the sort of young man who would help an old man do repairs around the house under the pretense that he, Bradley, needed to be taught how to do them *properly.* In short, Bradley was the sort of young man who was happiest when he was making other people happy, and other people were therefore happy whenever he appeared upon the scene.

There was, however, an unfortunate side effect to Bradley's general and universally agreed-upon delightfulness. Bradley, having grown up in a blessed cloud of good looks and sweet-temperedness, had never—despite all of Gretsella's best efforts—learned how to *think.* Whenever dear Bradley faced the merest difficulty, someone would notice his slight frown or heavy sigh and immediately swoop in to solve his problem for him, so he'd never been forced to simply grit his teeth and *figure it out* in the way that his fellow nonwitches often did. He sometimes floated through an entire day without having a single thought of any note, and he was perfectly capable of going an entire month before tallying up a full minute of earnest reflection.

This lack of thought made it somewhat difficult for Bradley to find himself a suitable profession. He first apprenticed himself to a blacksmith, imagining that he'd like to work with his hands, but after only a week, he abandoned the attempt on the grounds that the forge was too hot. Next, he tried to be a secretary at a local countinghouse, but he lasted only a fortnight before declaring himself sick to death of numbers and then quitting on the spot. When he arrived back at the cottage, Gretsella handed him a basket brimming with stinging nettles that needed to be stripped from their stems for her potion making. "If you refuse to find a profession of your own, then you'll do well enough as a witch's apprentice," she said.

The next day, Bradley apprenticed himself to the local hairdresser.

Working as a hairdresser suited Bradley. He had a natural gift for it, so he never had to bump up against the disagreeable sensation of having to truly apply himself. He got to work with his hands without having to sweat over a forge all day. The customers always had stories and gossip for him, so he was never bored. And, best of all, he got to make people happy by making them look their best. Making other people happy was all that Bradley needed to be happy, and—much as it pained her to admit it—Bradley's happiness was also Gretsella's chief source of joy. Seeing Bradley come through the front door of their cottage all smiles after having produced an especially flattering curl on the head of an especially difficult customer filled Gretsella with as much pride as the time she'd turned a particularly rude village mailman into a newt. Or with *more* pride, perhaps. As satisfying as the postal newtification had initially been, it had caused a great deal of chaos in the delivery of her packages.

Everything went smoothly until the evening of Bradley's eighteenth birthday. The day itself was perfectly pleasant:

Gretsella, to her great shame, spent the whole morning cooking and cleaning and wrapping Bradley's presents, which were some nice new boots and a pair of his very own haircutting shears. When he came home after work, the gifts were on the kitchen table next to a vase of flowers and a golden-brown roast chicken, and he immediately swept her up into a hug. "Oh, Mother, you didn't have to go to all of this trouble!"

"Don't be ridiculous," she said. "Sit down and eat your dinner before it gets cold." Then she took the opportunity of his sitting to wipe away a revoltingly sentimental tear.

The birthday dinner proceeded without incident. Bradley was effusive in his praise of the roast chicken and even more effusive in his thanks for the birthday presents, which he declared were exactly what he had wanted. He then started badgering Gretsella into letting him cut *her* hair. She bridled. "And what's *wrong* with my hair, young Bradley?"

"There's nothing wrong with your hair, Mother," Bradley said. "It's only that . . . well, it makes you look like a witch."

"And what's wrong with looking like a witch?" Gretsella asked, affronted.

"There's *nothing* wrong with it, Mother," Bradley said. "But you always complain about people stopping you when you're on your morning walks to ask you how to cast a spell to enchant their one true love."

Gretsella eyed him. Bradley gave her a very sweet smile. Gretsella, backed into a corner, scowled. "Oh, fine," she said. "In two minutes." Then she went out to use the outhouse, hoping that maybe he would get distracted by something like an attractive young woodsman walking past the cottage window and forget that his mother had made any promises.

Gretsella was walking back to the cottage when a bat swooped ominously past her head. This, in itself, was not unusual. It was dusk, after all, which was the proper time for vespertine pests. Gretsella, being a witch, approved of a nice traditional bat doing a bit of nice traditional ominous swooping. What was *entirely* untraditional was when the bat swooped past her head a second time and, in the voice of a horrible little man, screamed, "Hail, King Bradley! Hail to the One True King!"

"Oh, shut up," Gretsella hissed, and started furiously waving her hands through the air to try to fend it off. "Bradley doesn't want to be the king. Now go away! Shoo!"

"Mother?" Bradley said, poking his head out the door. He was already wearing his haircutting apron. "Who are you talking to? And why are you waving your hands in the air?"

"Don't you comment on a witch's business, young Bradley," Gretsella said, and swept back into the cottage, resolving to cast a spell in the morning that would make her home smell overwhelmingly of large, vicious bat-eating cats.

The next few days continued to present challenges to Gretsella's usual equilibrium. She was hounded at every turn by prophetic creatures of the forest, all of which seemed heaven-bent on relaying their dreadful tidings to her son. At first, she thought it was purely a mania that had seized the local bats, and that she would be safe so long as she kept Bradley indoors during the evening hours. This pleasant fantasy was brutally squelched the first time she went into the forest with Bradley to gather mushrooms and spied a squirrel sitting on a branch. The squirrel very clearly spotted Bradley at the same time. Its beady little eyes widened with shock, which Gretsella hadn't been aware was a facial expression available to squirrels. Then it dropped the acorn it was clasping, sat up on its furry haunches, and opened its mouth. It had just barely managed to get out a shrill "Hail!" when Gretsella flung a rock at it.

"Mother!" Bradley cried as the squirrel scampered away. "Why would you *throw a rock* at a squirrel? The poor animal didn't do a thing to you!"

"It hasn't done a thing to me *yet*," Gretsella said. "You never know what the filthy creatures might be planning." Then she grabbed ahold of Bradley's elbow to drag him away.

The squirrel, unfortunately, was far from the last of Gretsella's problems. That evening, Gretsella was forced to light a fire to smoke out an owl that was trying to hoot prophecies down the chimney, and she spent most of the following morning chasing a large family of chattery rabbits out of her garden before they could fill Bradley's dear, simple head with dangerous ideas about the role he ought to play in international geopolitics. She only felt entirely free to let her guard down when Bradley was at work. The hairdresser's shop was blessedly free of little woodland beasts who might attempt to crown him without his mother's consent.

After two weeks of this nonsense, Gretsella reached a day when she felt as if she had, perhaps, emerged victorious. She passed an entire blissful morning without any wretched animals attempting to disrupt her domestic tranquility with their relentless prophesizing. Then Bradley came home from work, and Gretsella knew immediately that something was afoot. In the nearly eighteen years of their acquaintance, she had never before seen Bradley with this particular expression on his face. He had the look of a young man who was, for the first time in his life, confronting a question that no one had been able to immediately resolve for him after a single glance at his delightful face. "Mother," he said, "a bunch of singing mice came into the shop from the back alley today."

"Singing mice!" Gretsella said, affecting utter astonishment. "Whoever heard of such a thing! I suppose that some high-spirited young witch must have been playing a practical joke." *Mice.* She hadn't even *considered* the possibility of Bradley being waylaid by a bunch of *mice.*

"A practical joke?" Bradley asked, looking distinctly relieved. "Do you really think that's it, Mother? They told me that I'm the *true king*!"

"Oh really, Bradley," Gretsella said. "A bunch of musical rodents barge into your workplace to sing songs about how you're the head of our national government, and your first response is to *believe* them? Don't you think that a practical joke is the more likely explanation?" She felt *slightly* guilty for misleading him like this, but it wasn't a very urgent feeling. Bradley would be much better off without all this king nonsense cluttering up the thus far blessedly well-ventilated space between his ears.

"You know, I think you're right," Bradley said. He looked more cheerful already. "How silly of me! I was starting to get awfully worried about it too. What would I do without you, Mother?"

"I have absolutely no idea," Gretsella said, and then they sat down for some tea and cake.

# A Short Story About Stories

Once upon a time, a moderately long time ago, a young woman who was doggedly trying to rid herself of the nickname Carrots fell painfully, desperately in love.

The object of Carrots's passion was a young man named Gareth who lived at the other end of the lane. He was a nice-looking boy, with big, sure hands that he used to milk his family's cows in the morning (he did this well but resentfully) and to strum his great-grandfather's lute in the evenings (he did this terribly but enthusiastically). He was a popular boy—not like Carrots—and so the first time he called out to her as she walked past his cottage, she looked behind her for the girl he was looking for. He wasn't looking for another girl, though, and she loved him for that like a sheepdog loves the shepherd.

Gareth would often walk down the lane to the cottage that Carrots lived in with her parents, lean against the garden fence, and talk to her about how he was going to leave home as soon as he turned sixteen and head straight to the city to seek his fortune. He and Carrots were both hazy about the details of how, exactly, a fortune was sought, let alone what one was supposed to do with it after it had been found, but that wasn't the point. The point was that he *wanted* to leave, wanted to go to faraway places and talk to fascinating people, possibly while drinking red wine and wearing a shirt with the buttons undone just past the point of masculine modesty. Listening to him talk made Carrots feel as if the world stood in front of her with its gates flung wide open. So she'd lean on one side of the garden fence, and he'd lean on the other, and once in a while they would kiss.

Carrots was a girl who read books. This was, most of the time, a wonderful thing. They broadened her perspective. They gave her things to think about other than herself. She loved stories, and she had faith in them in the way other people had faith in their own domestic gods. To a girl who believed in what she'd learned from stories, it felt lovely and gratifying but not particularly shocking that a handsome, popular young man could one day look at the girl who lived down the lane and suddenly, truly *see* her for the first time. This was what she thought had happened between her and Gareth, so she didn't hesitate for a moment to smile and wave and call out his name when he and three of his friends walked past her cottage one sunny afternoon.

He didn't smile back. He didn't wave. He looked at her with no expression at all, then looked away and said something to his friends. They all laughed. They didn't even stop walking.

Two things changed in Carrots that day.

The first change was that, somewhere deep in her appendix (the appendix being, in the folk tradition of Evermore, the organ said to excrete magic), a metaphorical gear ground into action.

The second was that, from then on, she had a certain amount of contempt for people who believed in silly romantic stories.

CHAPTER 2.5

# A Continuation of the Story That Was Interrupted by a Short Story About Stories

By the next day, Gretsella regretted having spent so much time fretting over the animals at all. Bradley seemed to have forgotten the tidings of the singing mice by suppertime, and having delivered their message, the animals seemed to have given up on making proclamations. Gretsella enjoyed another day without encountering a single wild creature emitting human speech, and Bradley came home chattering away about nothing but his customers and the latest village gossip. Life in Gretsella's cottage had returned to its natural rhythms, and it remained that way for a delightfully peaceful week, until Bradley came walking into the garden flanked by twenty armored men.

"Bradley!" Gretsella said. "Tell your friends to back up *this instant*—they're about to trample all over my rhododendrons."

To Gretsella's enormous satisfaction, several of the men

began to back up of their own accord. Bradley gave the men who remained a very sheepish little smile. "Would you mind awfully, fellows? My mother's very particular about the rhododendrons. She won a prize for them at the county fair last year."

This stern warning sent the rest of them back out to the lane, which gave Gretsella a chance to try to wrangle Bradley back into behaving exactly as she thought he should. "What on earth is going on, Bradley?" she asked, as if she didn't already suspect.

"These men are all knights from families still loyal to my father," Bradley said. He seemed to be in something of a daze. "They say that my father was the old king, which makes me the king now too. They want to accompany me to reclaim my throne."

"But you don't *have* a throne, Bradley," Gretsella said. "You're a *hairdresser.* What do you know about being a king?"

"They say that it's my destiny," Bradley said, though he was starting to look uncertain about it. "They say that the kingdom needs me in order for everything to return to balance and peace."

"That's the stupidest thing I've ever—" Gretsella started, then reined herself in. "What if you told them that you'd like to have the evening to think it over, hmm?"

"All right," Bradley said, and called out to the men. "I want to spend the evening alone to gather my thoughts. I'll speak to you all in the morning."

Gretsella had to admit that he *sounded* very kingly. The

men appeared to agree. There was a chorus of "Yes, Your Majesty," and the men withdrew. As soon as they were out of earshot, Bradley started to beam. "Did you hear, Mother? They call me *Your Majesty*!"

Gretsella suggested that he go to his room to spend the hours before dinner in earnest contemplation of the serious decision that lay before him. Then, once he was out of her way, she called an emergency convocation of her coven.

At any convocation held on such short notice, there was, inevitably, at least one member who sent her sincere regrets. This time it was Yarrow, which was unsurprising of the lazy old witch. Hyssop arrived early and nearly crash-landed in the rhododendrons: She wasn't used to flying her broom without her business partner serving as ballast near the bristles. Barb arrived pink-cheeked and sweaty, having just participated in something called a *Zumba class*. Upon further questioning, this was revealed to be a group of female villagers who joined Barb in rhythmic dancing beyond the reach of the oafish gazes of their husbands, which struck Gretsella as an almost *suspiciously* occultly correct sort of activity for Barb to partake in.

A few minutes later, Magnetia appeared, her face frozen in the hideous contortion of a woman about to sneeze. She had insisted on attending remotely, via magic mirror, despite the fact that Gretsella had explained *multiple* times that magic mirrors didn't work properly in her cottage. This had been the case ever since the mirror attached to Gretsella's bedroom vanity had provided Gretsella with its entirely unsolicited opinion on her physical attractiveness relative to that of a fourteen-year-old girl who lived in the village. Gretsella had informed the girl's father of the mirror's remarks, and he had taken Gretsella's old vanity down to the woodshed. He'd also built her a lovely new vanity with special compartments for all her unguents, so everything had, as usual, worked out perfectly for Gretsella. The sullen refusal of all other magic mirrors to thereafter operate reliably within Gretsella's home never would have been an issue if it weren't for Magnetia's *insistence* on being *modern*.

Gretsella, Hyssop, and Barb went ahead with their convocation as Magnetia's mirrored face jerked its way through a variety of rigid death masks. Gretsella poured tea. Barb opened a box of chocolate chip cookies that she freely admitted to having "just picked up on my way over." They were, as desserts, barely tolerable. Gretsella ate three of them as she explained the situation.

"This was all inevitable," declared Hyssop, who had a modest side business as a seer. She mostly predicted things that had already happened or were currently in the process of happening, but she did it with such verve that people paid her for it and recommended her to their friends.

"I—kind of thing—*traditional*," Magnetia said from the mirror before freezing again with her mouth partially open.

"I think it's fun!" Barb said. "What a nice opportunity for Bradley, since he decided against college."

"Witches' sons who live in cottages in the ancient forest don't go to *college, Barb*," Gretsella said. "And they don't become king either."

"Why not?" Barb asked. "Sometimes, all a kid needs is a little challenge to push them out of the nest. Melissa was a little adrift too, before she got certified to teach English abroad."

"Bradley," Gretsella said firmly, "is a simple, unspoiled boy who knows nothing of the world of men. He wouldn't enjoy a life in politics. Also, he'd be terrible at it. Possibly the worst king that Evermore has ever seen, even."

"Do you really think so?" Barb asked with a definite note of skepticism. "Worse than Horace the Disemboweler?"

"Worse—Edgar—the Handsy?" inquired the mirror-hobbled Magnetia.

"I understand completely," Hyssop said. "He lacks the *ruthlessness* needed for the position. Bradley's great-uncle Horack's not a man who's easily pushed around. Evermore would certainly be annexed by a neighbor almost immediately with Bradley at the helm. He would be too polite to vanquish the invaders."

"Exactly," Gretsella said. "Some warlord would very politely ask Bradley if he could stay at the palace for a week or two, and the next thing you know, we'd all be married to burly foreign horsemen."

"Oh," Magnetia said from her mirror. "Would—really—so bad?"

"You are a *witch*, young lady," Gretsella said, severely. It struck her that Magnetia and Bradley had a great deal in common when it came to burly horsemen. Baffling. Gretsella ate another cookie. Then she said, "I didn't call for this convocation so that you all could tell me what I ought to do. I called you so that you could assist me in pursuing what I've already determined is the correct course of action."

"As is traditional," Hyssop said. "How can we be of assistance?"

"I need ideas for how to convince a young man that he should be content to live at home with his mother," Gretsella said.

Hyssop shifted uncomfortably. Magnetia, for her part, was either frozen again or refraining from expressing an opinion.

All eyes turned toward Barb.

"Well," Barb said, "I don't think it's a very good idea to try to keep children from following their dreams. If you disapprove of something your child truly wants to do and try to discourage them, it can easily turn into a power struggle where you become the enemy, and they stick it out longer than they otherwise would because they don't want to give you the satisfaction of getting to say 'I told you so.' If I were you, I'd express my concerns once, very mildly, allow Bradley to make his own decisions, and be a sympathetic listening ear if and when things go badly."

"Interesting!" Gretsella said. "You have been very helpful, I'm sure. Convocation dismissed!" Then she set out to do exactly what she had planned on doing in the first place, which was to thoroughly convince Bradley of her obviously superior point of view.

She did her best, at least. She put forward her arguments.

She reminded Bradley of how much he liked working at the barbershop. She reminded him of how much he had disliked sitting in an office looking at paperwork, which she told him that she was certain a king would have to do day and night. She reminded him of the particularly handsome woodsman who had turned his head the previous week. She even considered dropping a little Oil of Enchantment into his soup, but ultimately decided against it; he had helped her brew potions since he was old enough to toddle, and thus would figure out what she'd done and be extremely annoyed with her the second the effects wore off. In short, she threw every last bit of her powers of motherly persuasion at the boy and went to bed fairly confident that she'd won him over to her point of view, a confidence that persisted until a knight in shining armor came riding into her garden.

It was as if he'd been made in a workshop as a weapon designed to test Bradley's resolve. He was square-jawed and broad-shouldered, and his hair brushed against said shoulders like an array of golden feather dusters. His eyes, even from a distance, were so clearly and provokingly blue that they looked as if they'd been painted on. Even his *horse* was handsome. "*Your Majesty!*" he called out. "*Your Majesty!*"

Within a few moments, Bradley, still in his bathrobe, was out the door as if he'd been spring-loaded. Gretsella assumed that he would want privacy while talking to the handsome knight, so she didn't follow him outside. She stayed inside the cottage and watched them through the curtains of the kitchen window instead.

She couldn't quite make out what they were saying. It certainly looked impassioned, whatever it was. At one point, the handsome knight got off his horse and then went down on his knees. "*A low blow, sir,*" Gretsella hissed at the window. Bradley looked fairly overcome. "*Stay strong, Bradley,*" Gretsella whispered, though she wasn't at all confident in Bradley's ability to maintain any kind of strength at all in the face of such a spectacle.

Just as she had expected, within a few minutes, Bradley came lolloping back into the cottage while the knight remounted his charger. Bradley's whole handsome, silly face was alight with newfound conviction. "Sir Harold has explained everything to me, Mother," he said. "I have to go reclaim my throne. The fate of the whole kingdom rests upon it."

"Is that so?" Gretsella asked. "How has Sir Harold's family been faring under the current government? I don't suppose that they're a mining family?" The current king had recently decreed a new sales tax on copper and iron.

"But what does that have to do with anything, Mother?" Bradley asked, looking genuinely perplexed. Then, before Gretsella could begin to explain, he said, "I have to pack my things. We're about to march to the capital."

"You're about to *what*?" Gretsella asked, but Bradley was already flitting off again.

CHAPTER 3

# In Which Gretsella Is Proven Right, as Usual

By later that afternoon, all Gretsella could do was watch, helpless, as her darling, dunderheaded son packed all of his earthly possessions into a small satchel. The army that was forming in her garden began to present a rapidly increasing danger to her delphiniums. At one point, Bradley picked up the scissors she'd given him for his birthday, then sighed and lovingly set them back in their rightful place. "I suppose that I won't need these once I'm king," he said.

"You don't *have* to be king," she said, but it was as if she hadn't said it at all.

He wrapped his arms around her and gave her a squeeze. "I promise to write every week."

At this point, to her great shame, Gretsella panicked. She wrenched herself out of Bradley's arms and darted into the back garden, where she snatched two toads out of her toad hole. What she was about to do would normally require a very involved bit of spellcasting, but today there was no time to waste. She threw both toads into a cold cauldron, did a bit of chanting at them, and then yanked them out again, hoping for the best.

"Here," she said, and thrust a toad toward Bradley. "It's for you."

Bradley received it very carefully and cradled it gently against his chest. "A toad," he said. "Thank you, Mother."

"It's a *toadaphone*," Gretsella said.

Bradley blinked at her. "Pardon?"

"A *toadaphone*," she repeated. "You can use it to speak with me as often as you want. Like this." She gave her toadaphone a firm pat on the head, then told it, "I'd like to speak to Bradley." After a brief pause, she said, "Hello, Bradley." A moment later, the toad that Bradley was holding said the same words in Gretsella's voice.

Bradley, to his great credit, didn't drop his toadaphone. Instead, he held it at arm's length, as if he thought it were about to spit venom in his eye, and said, "So I have to . . . slap the toad and then speak to it? And your toad will speak to you?"

"Toadaphone," Gretsella corrected. Her traitorous eyes were stinging. She resolutely refused to blink. "Don't go, Bradley. This is stupid."

"I *have* to go," Bradley said, and then gave his toadaphone a gentle little pat before tucking it into his pocket. "I'm going to name him Peepers."

"Witches never *name* their—" Gretsella started, then gave up. "Peepers is a very nice name. And I hope that the toadaphone will be useful. Sometimes they also give advice." She felt something absolutely horrible bubbling up within her, like a tentacled creature rising from the ocean floor to eat a cargo ship. That dreadful thing was the phrase *I love you*. She swallowed it back.

"I . . . tolerate you, Bradley," she said. "*Please* be careful."

"Oh, *Mother*," Bradley said, and gave her another big squeeze, along with a small sigh. "I love you too." Then he climbed onto a white horse and rode off to reclaim a throne that he hadn't even thought to be interested in a few days earlier.

# A Very Brief Digression on the Subject of Love

There are a certain number of people in the world who are at their best and happiest when they are alone. They roam across their private terrains like tigers, with the confidence of animals who know that no one else will ever steal the deer they want to eat for dinner. This sort of person will never waste a moment's time talking about how little they yearn for or need someone else, just as a tiger will never sit up and suddenly start talking about how a true apex predator would never need to hunt in a *pride*. The sorts of people who loudly declare that they're much too strong and independent and tough-minded to indulge in anything as gooey and irrational as *love* are, generally, the opposite of what they'd like to be. They're as delicate as ferns and as fragile as pigeons' eggs. Rejection of their love would be a blast of wiltingly hot summer air. It would crack them right open.

CHAPTER 3.5

# As We Were Saying

As soon as Bradley left, Gretsella began dedicating herself to cursemaking. It seemed as good a use of her current mood as anything else. There was a big county market coming up in a week, and cursed lavender sachets, which inflicted horrible nightmares upon sworn enemies or beloved husbands when placed under their pillows, always sold very briskly.

After finishing the sachets, Gretsella was collected enough in mind to start on more sedate work, such as the brewing of anti-itch potions and the sewing of little amulets that prevented the progression of baldness. It was enough to keep her busy for an entire week, during which time she absolutely did not spend any number of hours staring directly into the eyes of a toad, waiting for her son's voice to emerge from its warty mouth. Bradley, however, didn't call, and Gretsella refused to be the one to call him first. *She* wasn't the big, silly lunk who'd ridden off to the capital looking for a fight with the government; she didn't see why the sensible person in the equation should be the one to go begging for bits of information.

She also refused, on principle, to read the papers or listen to the old men gossiping about politics in the village square. She told herself that this was because she didn't want to reward Bradley's foolishness with her attention. If anyone had suggested to her that she was simply afraid of hearing bad news about her son, she would have refuted it. Gretsella was a strong, independent crone who had never been afraid of dark tidings in her entire life, and *furthermore*, Bradley wasn't *nearly* as dear as he imagined himself to be. When he did eventually call her, as she was certain he would, she would remind him of that fact to keep him humble.

Market day came and went. Gretsella sold out of nearly everything she'd made and earned a tidy profit. Ordinarily, she would celebrate a successful market day by buying herself some interesting new poisonous plants for her garden and making a special dinner for Bradley. On this market day, she simply headed home once it was over and went to bed.

AFTER BRADLEY HAD BEEN GONE FOR ALMOST A MONTH, Gretsella was finally forced to confront reality. She was taking a shortcut to the next village, walking along a footpath through a cow pasture and absolutely minding her own business, when an old woman of her acquaintance came hobbling up from the opposite direction. She was holding several enormous shopping bags. "Grandmother Gretsella!" she cried. "Such wonderful news about young Bradley!"

Though Gretsella appreciated the old woman's adherence to etiquette, it always threw her into a momentary fog of confusion whenever someone considerably older than she was addressed her as "Grandmother." Whoever had established the protocol for addressing witches had clearly not taken into account the fact that elderly ladies who were *not* witches also existed and might occasionally need to address one of their more magical peers in a way that wasn't extremely confusing to everyone involved. Gretsella was so caught up in this thought, and the woman's speech was so garbled (she was of such advanced years that she was in possession of what appeared to be no more than three remaining teeth, two at the bottom and one at the top), that it took her a moment to register what had been said. "*What* about young Bradley?"

"Why, his glorious victory over the usurper!" the old woman said.

Gretsella stared at her. The old woman beamed toothlessly back, like a dim-witted duck that had just been presented with a loaf of very soft bread. Gretsella took a moment to resent her with an enormous fullness of spirit. Then she said, "That sounds *very* unlikely, madam."

"But it's true! Every word!" the old woman said. "Haven't you seen it in the papers?"

"I," Gretsella said, with dignity, "am a *witch*. We see the past, present, and future in the bottoms of our cauldrons. We do not *read the papers*."

"What's that?" the old woman asked.

Gretsella gritted her teeth and repeated herself.

"Well," the old woman said, "didn't you see it in your cauldron, then?"

Gretsella glared at her. The old woman smiled gummily back. "I elected not to check," Gretsella said loudly. "Don't you need to get home with your shopping?" A cold wind began to whip through the pasture.

The old woman didn't seem to notice Gretsella's subtle witchly signals of displeasure. "It said in the papers that his men stormed the castle, and Bradley himself knocked out the usurper with a single right hook!"

His right hook. *Barb*. Her blessed gift had brought trouble after all, just as Hyssop had predicted. Dark clouds began to roll in. "Oh, Barb!" Gretsella cried, and raised her hands above her. A bolt of lightning cut across the clouds. "By earth and hemlock, by cat's blood and bat's wing, in the name of my witchmothers, I curse you, Barb!"

"The weather is *very* changeable at this time of year!" the old woman remarked, and pulled an enormous umbrella from one of her shopping bags.

"I hope that your top tooth falls out and that your porridge oats don't cook through," Gretsella hissed, then turned away to stomp home to her cottage.

"His coronation is in a week!" said the old woman, who was now trotting along by Gretsella's side at a truly extraordinary speed. "Here, share my umbrella, Grandmother. It really does look like rain."

Gretsella groaned.

SHE SPENT A FEW MORE DAYS AFTER THAT NURSING HER wounds and refusing to call Bradley. Why *should* she call him when he hadn't bothered to pick up his toad and tell his own mother that he was about to be crowned king? So she waited, and sulked, and then when the day of the coronation arrived, she tracked down her toadaphone (which was hopping around in the garden), gave it a brisk pat on the head, and said, "I would like to speak to Bradley. Bradley, how are you?"

There was no response. Gretsella waited for a few minutes, then gave up, set the toad down, and decided to do some weeding. Buttercups were springing up in her stinging nettle patch. She contemplated sending Bradley some nettles in the mail. A fistful of stinging nettles might remind the boy of where he had come from. It would probably be useless, though. He probably had *servants* to open his suspicious packages for him.

"Hello, Mother!" said Bradley's voice from somewhere near Gretsella's right ankle.

She nearly fell forward into her nettle patch. Then she nearly fell backward onto her toadaphone. Then she snatched up the toad and said, "Bradley! Hello! Are you well? I've heard that you're the king!" It was an extremely stupid thing to say. She regretted it immediately.

"I'm *wonderful*," Bradley said. He sounded a bit funny. He sounded *drunk*, Gretsella realized after a moment. Bradley wasn't usually the sort of young man who liked to drink more than a glass or two. He also wasn't usually the sort of young man who liked to overthrow the government, so Gretsella supposed that she shouldn't make assumptions.

"We're having a party!" It certainly sounded like it: There was a great deal of clamor in the background. "Everyone here is *awfully* nice to me, Mother."

"I'm glad to hear it," Gretsella said, though she most certainly was not. If they were *less* nice to him, he would be more likely to *come home*. "And . . . congratulations. On . . . this *king* nonsense. I suppose."

"Thank you, Mother," Bradley said. "I shall endeavor to be the very best king that this land has ever seen!"

"Who told you to say that?" Gretsella asked, immediately suspicious.

"*Ooh*, there's jugglers!" Bradley said, and the toad went silent.

Gretsella frowned. "Bradley?" Maybe she shouldn't have been quite so suspicious. Maybe she ought to have expressed more sincere congratulations on his victory. Maybe, as his mother, she ought to have said that she was proud. "Are you there, Bradley?"

The toad said, "Ribbit."

"There's no call for *sarcasm*," Gretsella said, and put the toad into the nettle patch as its punishment for cheek.

FOR THE NEXT FEW WEEKS, GRETSELLA FOUND HERSELF FEELing distinctly displeased. She refused to call it *sad*. Witches didn't just wander around in their nightgowns eating chocolate cake and *feeling sad*, so that obviously *couldn't* be what Gretsella was doing. *Brooding*, she called it. She brooded. She did it wickedly. She invented several exciting new curses, including one particularly fiendish little number that afflicted its subject with hiccups whenever they attended a wedding, a funeral, or the sort of concert that included lots of long, solemn pauses in order to trick the audience into applauding.

She missed Bradley. The toadaphone hopped through the garden in silence.

A few months passed. Then, one day, Barb appeared on Gretsella's doorstep. She was wearing a sleeveless pink dress and holding a Bundt cake. "Hello, Gretsella," she trilled. "I was just in the neighborhood and thought I'd drop by."

"With a *cake*?" Gretsella asked. "Didn't you notice that I cursed you?"

"Well, yes," Barb said. "But I didn't want to take it too personally. I assumed that you were just upset over Bradley moving out." She eyed Gretsella's hair, which hadn't been brushed for a span of time considerably longer than what even witches generally found acceptable. A witch might deliberately cultivate the impression that she *might* have bats nesting in her hair, but most witches drew the line at the point when small animals really did start getting trapped in the snarls. "May I come in?"

Gretsella glared at her. "What kind of cake is it?"

"Lemon," Barb said. "With a lavender glaze."

"I curse you once more, Barb," Gretsella mumbled, and stepped aside to let Barb in. The wicked old hag *knew* that Gretsella couldn't resist a lavender glaze.

They sat down for tea and cake in Gretsella's living room. Barb served Gretsella a very large slice, which Gretsella gobbled down almost in one gulp while trying not to look visibly sad, like a python going through a difficult breakup. Barb looked alarmed. Then she said, "You know, I'm a little worried about Bradley. Did you hear that he's canceled the taxes?"

Gretsella blinked. "Which taxes?"

"That's just the thing," Barb said. She took a dainty bite of cake, chewed, and swallowed. Then she took a sip of tea. "According to the papers, it's *all* of the taxes."

"Oh Bradley," Gretsella said. She really didn't know what was going to happen to the boy, and she didn't at all like the way the tea leaves were swirling. Briefly, she considered whether the economic depression that the nation had surely just entered would present a good opportunity to apply for a low-interest mortgage on a new cottage, one with enough space for a dedicated studio for her arts and crafts projects (like cursed amulets and little dolls with authentic human teeth). Then she remembered *who* had probably single-handedly crashed the stock market, and sighed. "Barb, he's an *idiot*."

Barb, wisely, chose not to respond to this directly. "More cake?"

The matter of the taxes nagged at Gretsella a bit. It was such a ridiculous, birdbrained—*Bradley*-brained—thing to do. It was, she imagined, the kind of thing that some sort of adviser with a long white beard and whatever passed for wisdom among the menfolk should have told him not to do, but apparently no such adviser had bothered.

She would have told him what was what if *she* were his adviser, but he'd left her behind when he marched off to the capital.

She considered cursing him. She settled on continuing to refuse to call him first.

She had come fairly close to reestablishing a comfortable, cozy, Bradley-free routine for the first time in eighteen years when, a few days after her visit from Barb, she heard sobbing coming from her back garden.

She went back there to investigate and found the sobbing emanating from her toadaphone. She fished it out of the nettle patch—it had taken a worrying liking to the nettles—and spoke to the toad. "Bradley!" she said. "What is it, darling?" Then she blinked and resolved to dose herself at bedtime with a strong potion that would prevent her from ever again uttering the word *darling*.

"Everything is absolutely awful," Bradley cried, and then the toad was forced to produce a number of loud thumping and rustling noises, which Gretsella could only assume were the consequence of Bradley having dramatically flung himself onto his kingly four-poster.

"I'm so terribly sorry to hear that," Gretsella said, though this was a bold and wicked falsehood. She wasn't sorry to hear it at all. She was, in fact, very pleased to hear it, due to her presumption that the more miserable Bradley became, the more likely he was to forget about all of this ridiculous king business and come home.

She didn't say anything to that effect aloud, of course. She was far too sly a crone for that. Instead, she carried her toad back into the cottage and set it on the countertop so that she could make a pot of tea while they talked. She suspected that this might take a while. "Tell Mother all about it."

Bradley told her all about it. She wasn't wrong about it taking a while: Bradley had a whole litany of complaints to recite woefully from under his blankets (she was sure he was hiding from his courtiers under the covers). The Treasury was running dry, and the queen of Overthere was threatening to call in Evermore's debts. The crops were failing in the South, and streams of hungry peasants were setting up tent cities in the capital. There were rumors of insurrection from a number of noble families in the North. And, worst of all, the handsome knight who had whisked Bradley off in the first place had lately been seen canoodling with one of Bradley's kitchen maids. "What am I going to do, Mother?" he asked her, his voice somewhat muffled by goose down and despair. "Peepers keeps shouting at me about how I'm going to cause the downfall of the kingdom!"

"That's very odd," Gretsella said. "Toadaphones don't usually prophesize independently. Maybe it has to do with the climate at the capital." More likely, it had something to do with the hasty way in which Gretsella had enchanted the toad, but she certainly wasn't going to tell Bradley *that*. "Don't you have any wise advisers to tell you what to do?" she asked, then got up and went to her closet to pull out her long-neglected suitcase.

"No!" Bradley said. "They all left when I drove off my great-uncle, the usurper! There's no one here who's half as wise as you!"

"Oh dear," Gretsella said, examining her best black dresses for moth holes before carefully folding them and packing them into the suitcase. "It does sound very difficult to be all alone there, with no one you trust to advise you."

"It *is*, Mother," the dejected Bradley said.

"And with your having been so accustomed to being able to ask *me* for advice," Gretsella said as she packed a few pairs of clean stockings. The trick with Bradley, she had found, was to keep gently herding him toward the conclusion at which you wanted him to arrive, for significantly longer than you originally expected would be necessary. He would get there eventually, given enough time.

"Oh, Mother!" Bradley said then, his voice gone suddenly brighter. "That gives me an idea! Why don't you come to the capital and be my chief adviser?"

"Why, what an *idea*, Bradley!" Gretsella said. "I never would have thought of it. Do you really think I might be helpful? I don't know anything about running a kingdom." She would go there by stagecoach, she thought, for the sake of comfort, but she would also bring her collapsible broomstick in case of accidents on the highway.

"Oh, *please* come, Mother," Bradley said. "You're the smartest person I know. I'm sure you'll be able to help me out of this mess."

"Well, if you really think so, Bradley," Gretsella said, consulting her crystal ball to see when the first coach was leaving town the next morning, "I suppose I might be able to come and do my best to advise you."

CHAPTER 4

# In Which Gretsella Gets to Work

Gretsella very soon regretted her decision to take a stagecoach to the capital. The highway was extremely pitted—far worse than she remembered it being when she'd last made this trip as a starry-eyed young witch embarking on a journey to visit the execution grounds of various Great Witches of History—and they were still several miles outside the capital when traffic came to an abrupt and total halt. She waited for half an hour while growing increasingly impatient with the insipid conversations of her fellow passengers—what sort of unbalanced personality could possibly have so much to say about a *wedding*?—until she finally gave up, unfolded her collapsible broomstick, and took flight.

Traveling by broomstick, in addition to being more convenient than being trapped in a stagecoach, provided Gretsella with a sweeping view of the current state of the city. The state of the city did not appear to involve much in the way of glistening palaces on the hill, prancing unicorns, or anything else that Bradley might have expected to encounter when he rode off to rule his kingdom. There were lots of tents in the public squares. Gretsella, though not an expert in urban environments, suspected that this was not the intended use of the squares in question. It certainly struck her as somewhat untraditional to stock the squares with poor and desperate people living in tents, instead of poor and desperate people who had formed an angry mob in order to indulge in a bit of rotten-egg-throwing, witch-dunking, or politician-beheading. As far as Gretsella was concerned, watching poor and desperate people violently get the best of the upper classes was one of the chief joys of a city vacation, but watching poor and desperate people sit around sadly next to the statue of a naked woman who was supposed to represent the Spirit of Charity could only suffuse one with the Spirit of Melancholy.

# Interlude: An Excerpt from a Tourist's Guide to the Capital of Evermore

The first thing noticed by most visitors to the bustling capital of the Kingdom of Evermore is what the city lacks. The capital, which is the economic, cultural, and political center of the kingdom, doesn't have a name. This is because of, and not despite, the city's storied history.

The capital of Evermore was initially called Warrockston, after the ancient warrior-king who, it is said,[1] discovered a spring of sweet water when he thrust his sword into the ground at the end of a long battle and decided to build a fortress on the spot. Despite having been married seven times before his prolonged and unpleasant death from poisonous

---

1 It isn't said by anyone who has even a slight familiarity with the archeological record, but it's definitely said.

atmospheric vapors,[2] Warrock never managed to produce a legitimate heir, and his death resulted in a lengthy war between factions led by his chief adviser, his younger brother, and his eldest son, Horace the Unacknowledged. Horace emerged the victor and, in an act of bracing spitefulness, moved the seat of government to a rural hunting lodge and gave Warrockston a new name: Bastordston.[3]

Horace was instructed by his advisers to shore up his strategic alliances, so he married a highly educated foreign princess, who quickly came to the conclusion that her only hope of finding someone capable of holding a conversation in the entire Kingdom of Evermore was to give birth to and then educate that person herself. She had eight children, all of whom could speak five languages and still never talked to their father if they could possibly avoid it. Horace's eldest son, Hiram the Extremely Learned, promptly moved back to the capital before his own coronation and renamed it Meddonoloparpanell, which means "Place of Continuous Virtue" in Old High Evermorish.[4] After *his* death, *his* son, Morton the Prac-

---

2 Syphilis.

3 Being illegitimate, Horace had not enjoyed the privilege of a princely education and was not very good at spelling. He was, however, very good at having people's heads put onto spikes, so no one ever corrected him.

4 Old High Evermorish was only ever spoken by a few members of Evermore's ancient tribal nobility, and it is notoriously nearly impossible to learn. In modern Evermore, a small guild of about half a dozen scholars of Old High Evermorish charges exorbitant fees to anyone who wants an

tical, ruthlessly abbreviated the name to the nonsensical (and vaguely flatulent) Parpo. And so it went, king after king, until the people of Evermore quietly gave up on remaking their signs and maps every few years and started to refer to the capital as, simply, the Capital. Patriotic citizens of Evermore will often, while abroad, attempt to convince patriotic citizens of other countries that adding "of Evermore" after "the Capital" is a type of mispronunciation. This usually doesn't go over very well, but the people of Evermore aren't known for their cultural sensitivity.[5]

**END OF INTERLUDE**

---

impressive-looking runic inscription for a gravestone or marriage certificate or family coat of arms. Cynics have suggested that the members of this guild are wily old frauds who've made up a bunch of interesting-looking scribbles in order to sell fake cultural heritage to upwardly mobile types, and that true Old High Evermorish, if it ever existed, has long since died and been completely forgotten. Less cynical Evermorians suspect that the cynics might be onto something, but they like how the genuine reproduction ancient tablet they bought looks on the mantelpiece, so try not to think about it too deeply.

5 They're known mostly for hard cheeses, and for the kind of traditional folk dancing that's both uninteresting to watch and exhausting to participate in for longer than almost exactly one and a half minutes.[6]

6 One of the most famous traditional Evermorish folk dances is called Luulabennagalbolein, which in Old High Evermorish means "dance in which we wave heavy wooden clubs in very slow circles over our heads until we feel tired."[7]

7 Allegedly. See note four.

GRETSELLA LANDED VERY NEAR THE PALACE, THEN TUCKED her broom back into her suitcase, marched up to the palace's huge iron gate, and announced, "I'm here to see Bradley." The guards ignored her. She repeated herself more loudly. "I'm *here* to see *Bradley.*"

The guards deigned to look at her. "Who?"

"*Bradley,*" she said. "Oh, for wickedness' sake. The *king.*"

"Move along, old woman," one of the guards said.

"All right," Gretsella said, and marched on through the gate.

The guards had evidently not expected this, because it took them a moment to leap after her. She evaded them very neatly for a minute or so—she had enchanted her shoes for light-footedness—but alas, one of them had very long arms. He grabbed hold of her. Gretsella would later maintain that she turned him into a parrot *entirely* in self-defense.

The parrot squawked. So did his colleague, who turned around to sprint away from Gretsella at a truly impressive speed. "Witch!" he screamed. "Witch!"

"Yes, exactly," Gretsella said. "And let that be a lesson to you!" Then she started walking toward the palace steps again. She had made it almost the rest of the way there when an enormous net descended upon her, followed by the full weight of a very large and very heavy guard. Gretsella said, "*Oof.*"

"We've got you now, witch!" the guard said. A large crowd of armed men was now gathered around her. Gretsella tried to aim a spell through the holes in the net and nearly singed her own finger off.

"Wizard work," she hissed, disgusted. She didn't approve of wizards. They were mostly men, and generally more satisfied with themselves than Gretsella thought that a man ought to be.

"Take her to the dungeon!" the leader of the guards cried.

"Oh, for the love of *brimstone*," Gretsella said, and tried to wriggle her way free, but it was no use: The anti-witch net held firm, and the guards carted her off to the dungeon like a wild boar about to be made very intimate with some heirloom carrots and new potatoes.

They threw her, net and all, into a cell in the dungeon, then left her to her own devices. Her first device was to wriggle her way out of the anti-witch net. Her second device was to turn herself into a mouse and creep out of her cell and into the palace walls.

Gretsella climbed upward along the path of a drainpipe, passing a number of grand, empty rooms coated in dust. Then, eventually, she came to a room occupied by a young woman who appeared to be busily packing everything she owned into a suitcase. She was about Gretsella's size. Gretsella made her mouse's head into a tiny version of her own head in order to speak, and immediately regretted the choice. It was very awkward, and also objectively disgusting. "Excuse me," she said. "I'm the king's mother, and I would like to borrow a dress."

The young woman looked up and, to her credit, let out only a very brief and muted scream. "You don't look like the king's mother," she said after she'd taken a moment to recover. "You look like a hideous tiny cheese-eating nightmare fiend."

"That may be so," Gretsella said. "But it isn't very polite of you to mention it. Just be a good girl and bring a dress over here."

The girl threw a dress in Gretsella's general direction. Gretsella crawled into the garment and expanded herself into her usual human form to fit it, which created a very uncomfortable sensation, particularly in the area of the tail. Once she was sufficiently expanded, she gave the girl a nod. "Hello. What's your name, who are you, and where are you going? I didn't know that there were other witches in the palace." Gretsella *hated* not knowing things. This girl was certainly a witch, though, if perhaps one still in the larval stage. It wasn't anything about how she looked, exactly. She was a very ordinary-looking girl, if a bit gawky, with limp brown hair and light-brown eyes and little brown freckles on her nose.

"I'm not a witch, and I don't see how any of that's any of *your* business," the girl said. Then she hastily added, "That is to say, I wouldn't want to annoy you by going on and on about my silly problems, Grandmother." She was smart enough to know how to properly address a witch, even if she was pretending that she wasn't one herself. This was a fairly usual phase in the lives of some young witches, though Gretsella had always thought it a fairly embarrassing one. Refusing to embrace one's own inherent witchliness was like going back to the shop and earnestly telling the cashier that he'd given you too much change.

"I would say that everything in the palace is my business," Gretsella said. Then she added importantly, "My son, Bradley—the king—asked me to come and help him straighten things out around here." Gretsella had never cared about all of the vast riches that might accompany Bradley's new title, but in this moment, she realized she very much enjoyed being able to wield the power of the throne purely to satisfy her own unquenchable nosiness.

"Oh," the girl-who-claimed-she-wasn't-a-witch said. "Oh, well, I guess it doesn't matter what I tell you. I was the court jester, but the new king fired me, so now I'm packing up and heading home to Northwind County to sing songs about merry accommodating maidens until I drop dead of ennui." She shoved a fistful of underthings into her bag without stopping to fold them. "And my name's Janet. Janet Findimatabar." Then, in response to the look on Gretsella's face, she added, "My father always told me that our surname came from my great-great-grandfather, whose exploits made him famous in all of the surrounding counties."

"Hmm," Gretsella said. "Sounds just like a man. And Northwind County, you say? That's not far from Brigandale, is it?"

Janet blinked. "Brigandale? Yes. I grew up there, actually, but there aren't enough taverns in the forest to make a living there as a wandering minstrel. Not that you can make much of a living at it in Northwind County either."

Gretsella gave a satisfied nod. It made sense that the girl had been raised in Brigandale. Gretsella could easily recognize an essentially witchy disposition when she was wearing its dress. "There's always apprenticing yourself to a witch, if you're considering a change of careers," she said. Sometimes a young witch simply needed a little nudge in the right direction to be saved from a life of unwitchly delinquency.

"I don't *want* to be a witch," Janet said. "All of those nasty potions and things, and having to live alone in the woods. Begging your pardon, Grandmother. I like living at court. I like all of the gossip and scheming. Or I *liked* it, until the king fired me."

"Why on earth would Bradley *fire* you?" Gretsella asked, genuinely perplexed by the very idea. She was fairly sure that Bradley didn't have the cold-bloodedness necessary to fire someone, especially if it seemed as if they might be *sad* about it or—horror of horrors—shed a tear or two.

"He thought that I jested too cruelly," Janet said. "I don't think that my jesting was *cruel*. It was just ordinary jesting."

"Oh dear," Gretsella said. "I think that I'm beginning to understand. Did you say something that might have made someone feel a little badly, in the course of your jesting?"

Janet stared at her as if she thought Gretsella might have recently been clobbered over the head. "That's the whole *point*," she said. "You're supposed to ridicule the foibles of king and court. What *else* is a jester supposed to do?"

"I don't know," Gretsella said. "Bradley's *sensitive*. He must have been born that way. He didn't get it from *me*." She pondered for a moment. "Was it *Bradley* whose foibles you ridiculed?"

"Oh, he never minded that," Janet said. "It was when I made jokes about that awful, self-satisfied Sir Harold always chasing after the kitchen maids."

"Ah," Gretsella said. "Bradley was probably suffering from an acute attack of jawline-induced mental collapse. He has them every six months or so. As far as I can tell, the condition's incurable." She adjusted the sleeves of her newly borrowed dress. An ordinary adjustment didn't quite suffice, so she moved a bit of very confused matter from the window curtains to make her sleeves half an inch longer. Then she said, "Come on. We'll just have to tell him to hire you back."

Janet trotted along after her agreeably enough as Gretsella headed out into the hall. "Are you sure that you'll be able to convince him to do it, Grandmother?" she asked. "He seemed pretty determined about firing me, though he was very polite about it."

"Of course," Gretsella said. "Bradley is always polite. And he's usually fairly reasonable once you've explained things to him clearly."

"I see," Janet said. "But won't he worry about whether or not you're thinking straight when you suddenly appear in front of him without any shoes or stockings on?"

Gretsella looked down at her bare toes and gave them a brief wiggle. Her cheeks went slightly warm. "We witches *never* wear shoes when we're working our most powerful magics," she declared in an authoritative tone that she hoped Janet would find convincing. "Now, where will we find Bradley?" Her sleeves, as she spoke, twitched. There was a draft coming through the window frame at the other end of the room, and the late curtains weren't sure whether or not they ought to billow.

Janet led her through the palace to a room that Gretsella could only assume was the great hall, as it was very large and very long and very full of people who appeared to be courtiers doing something that could only be described as *feasting*. Bradley was sitting at the very head of the table, looking deeply glum.

When he saw Gretsella, he beamed and leapt to his feet. "Mother! You really came!"

"Of course I did," Gretsella said as she withstood the onslaught of embraces that Bradley shortly began to rain upon her. "I'm a *witch*." She didn't add that a witch's word was her bond (except when she was lying). She thought that went without saying. "You look terrible."

"Oh, I've just been feeling a little low," Bradley said. "But I'm much better now that you're here. I'll tell the servants to throw you a feast of welcome!" Then he glanced to the side and noticed Janet. "Miss Janet! What are you doing here? I beg your pardon, but I am positive that I fired you just a few hours ago. Is something the matter?"

Janet briefly attained the somewhat flustered glow that Bradley often incited in young ladies when he was beaming attentive politeness at them out of his bewilderingly handsome face. Then she gathered herself and cleared her throat. "Oh, yes, uh . . . your mother wanted to speak to you. About that."

"We'll go somewhere private," Gretsella declared, and marched them both smartly out of the room.

"Oh dear, Mother," Bradley said. "What happened to your shoes?"

"Never mind, Bradley," Gretsella said. "We have more important things to discuss. I need you to hire Janet back."

Bradley frowned. "It's a little delicate, Mother," he said. "I did feel awful for firing her, but she was being *rude* to my guests." He said the last bit of that sentence in a hushed whisper, as if he were describing having caught the court jester engaged in unwholesome communion with a jam jar.

"It's not rudeness if it's in the course of *jesting*, Bradley," Gretsella said.

Bradley's expression took on the vague, abstracted quality it always took on when someone tried to explain to him why, say, a pound of feathers weighed the same as a pound of lead. Then he brightened. "Oh," he said. "Like how if it's *art*, it's not *naked*."

"*Exactly* like that, Bradley," Gretsella said. "What a perfect way of putting it."

Bradley beamed. Gretsella went in for the killing blow. "And, you know, all of the most fashionable courts have jesters. Magnetia was telling me so just the other day. It would look funny if you were the only king who *didn't* have a jester."

"Your lady mother is right, Your Majesty," Janet put in. "As your jester, I'm also sworn to relay all of the court gossip back to you, so that you can never be taken off guard by treachery. It's a very important role, Your Majesty. As your loyal subject, I feel that it's my duty to urge you to hire another jester as soon as possible. That way, you won't be left without an essential member of your palace staff."

"*And*," Gretsella added before Bradley's poor overheated brain had any time to percolate any stray thoughts, "if you keep Janet as your jester, she'll be able to provide entertainment at my feast tonight."

Just as Gretsella had anticipated, the mention of a party perked Bradley up immediately. "I suppose that's right," he said. "It *is* nice to have music at a party."

"Exactly. Good! It's settled, then," Gretsella said, and moved on to the next subject without giving Bradley the chance to contemplate what had just transpired. "And I'll need you to send someone into the dungeon to get my things."

"But what on earth are your things doing in the dungeon, Mother?" Bradley asked with great evident astonishment.

"Never you mind, Bradley," Gretsella said, and within two minutes, King Bradley was happily sending his servants scurrying hither and yon in service to every one of Gretsella's wicked ends.

CHAPTER 5

# In Which Gretsella Surveils the Terrain

After Gretsella was fully dressed in her own clothes again, and Bradley fully and joyfully engaged in planning the welcome party, Gretsella decided to make a more complete survey of her new domain. She started at the bottom, in the kitchen, which she thought ought to be considered the most important part of any house. One could easily do without a sitting room—indeed, being able to honestly claim that an unfortunate workplace accident had caused one's sitting room to sink into a flaming sulfureous pit was just the ticket for warding off a sudden infestation of *guests*—but no self-respecting witch could do without a kitchen. A witch needed a nice, clean, modern kitchen for making potions. And pies (when protected from the prying eyes of members of the public, who were better off believing that witches subsisted on midnight mists and salamander tongues). Gretsella did like a nice piece of pie.

As soon as Gretsella made it into the kitchen, she could tell that there was something gravely amiss. The entire atmosphere of the room was wrong. A large kitchen should be hot and loud and full of people rushing around through banks of good-smelling steam and getting cursed at by the head cooks and burning their hands on scalding pans and generally suffering enormously for the sake of quivering aspics and golden loaves of bread and roasts dripping fragrant grease all over enormous mounds of crispy potatoes. This kitchen had the screaming, rushing, and suffering, but all of this seemed to be in service to nothing but chaos itself. As a philosophically *wicked* witch, Gretsella approved. As a witch who looked forward to a nice supper in the evenings, she didn't approve in the slightest.

There were a number of figures prominent to the scene. The one who first drew Gretsella's eye was propped against a barrel in a corner near the stove. He was pale and long and thin, and bundled up with an old-fashioned kerchief tied around his neck, as if he were suffering from a chill. He was smoking a large pipe in a way that suggested the effort exhausted him. A nearly empty bottle of wine stood at his right elbow, while at his left sat a shorter, stouter man with whom he was engaged in an extremely languorous game of whist. Around these two bolted a number of young women and younger boys, all pursued by a large woman who kept shouting things like "Is *that* what you call a clean pot?" after them. At one point, one of the young boys tripped over the thin man's legs, and one of the girls lifted the boy to his feet and hurried him along as if he'd tripped over a tree root. It seemed, in fact, as if everyone in the room were doing their best to pretend that the thin man wasn't there at all—except for the large woman, who kept casting scornful glances at him and then sighing like a dog lying down on a rug.

# A Digression on the Subject of Colorful Minor Characters

A highly reliable characteristic of books is that characters the protagonist briefly encounters in passing tend to be, on the whole, much more entertaining than the protagonist himself. This can be blamed on a few basic difficulties with the ways that a story functions. The first is that the protagonist has a lot of plot to accomplish, so he can't waste too much time bumbling, prancing, or making merry japes when he's busy being forced to fight his fellow prisoners to the death in the gladiatorial arena (this being a fate that befalls protagonists at a rate an astonishing 4,500 percent higher than it does the general population). The second is that the kind of bumbling, japes, et cetera that amuse the reader for a few paragraphs can become irritating when extended over several hundred pages. The third is that the author has fallen so deeply and thoroughly in love with her protagonist that, like the doting mother of a jaundiced and cross-eyed infant, she assumes that his charms are self-explanatory, and thus fails to make them clear within the narrative itself. The fourth is that everyone, including writers of stories, has gotten so used to protagonists never being red-faced cooks dressed in floury aprons that it never occurs to them to write one that way.

The fifth reason is the very worst to contemplate. The terrible truth is that protagonists are written to be how we would like to imagine ourselves, and the colorful side characters are how we fear we look to other people. Here we are, striding around accomplishing all of our very important tasks, thinking complicated and nuanced thoughts about politics and mortality and our relationships with our mothers. There we go, driving with skill and precision, making love in a way that nearly brings our partners to tears of ecstasy, and parrying any insults with exquisitely witty ripostes. How cruel, how monstrous it would be if we were forced to see ourselves as we're afraid other people do: as that sloppy woman in a wrinkled dress who broke a lull at a party with a tasteless, too-loud joke; as that pompous man with thinning hair who cut someone off in traffic the other day and ruins first kisses with the erratic thrusting of his tongue; as that preposterous personage who persists in wearing unflattering hats and drawing mediocre pictures in coffee shops, all the while hoping that someone will notice and think, *Ooh, how interesting!*

We are all, as horrible as it is to contemplate, colorful minor characters, walking around with a pimple on our chin that we hope no one notices, with one patch that we forgot to shave, with a strange-sounding sneeze, with coffee breath. We're all stuck here, exposed like turtles on high rocks, forced to live out every day without even the smallest quests or prophecies to wrap around our deficiencies and make them into something meaningful. What a mercy it is to open a book and briefly become the hero, our flaws adding depth and complexity to our character, our mistakes only serving to heighten the narrative tension, our quiet terror that we're too insignificant to matter at all submerged, if only for a moment, in the rushing river of a story.

CHAPTER 5.5

# Back to the Kitchen We Abandoned in Pursuit of the Most Recent Digression

Into this tableau drifted Gretsella, attempting to look like someone who had wandered into the kitchen in pursuit of the scent of freshly baked dinner rolls and had absolutely no secret political motivations whatsoever. As she always felt confident in everything she did, she felt entirely confident that she was succeeding in her gambit, and remained cheerfully oblivious to the skeptical glances being cast at her from every direction until the stout woman placed herself directly in Gretsella's path and said, "We're not hiring anyone, and we're not buying anything."

"I haven't brought anything to sell, and I've never worked an honest day in my life," Gretsella said proudly, if inaccurately (like most witches, she had spent some time in the service industry before she was able to support herself with her witchcraft full-time). "I am Gretsella, King Bradley's mother."

Gretsella watched with interest as everyone within earshot began flapping around like bats trying to escape from a chimney. There was such a mass adjusting of aprons that it kicked up a breeze.

"I most *humbly* beg your pardon, madam," the stout woman said, with gratifying obsequiousness. "How might we be of service to you, madam?"

"I just wanted to have a little chat," Gretsella said. "And some coffee and cake, I think."

"Of *course*, madam," the stout woman said. Then she hissed, "In the office!" at the nearest hapless young person before leading Gretsella through a discreet door in the corner.

The office was a small, dark, uncomfortable room with lots of very large furniture crammed into it and a strong smell of stale tobacco in the air. It must have once been the den of a *man*, Gretsella imagined: Men were known for their love of dark corners and stagnant air. It was also extremely messy, as if someone had been rummaging around for something and then neglected to put anything back in its place.

"I'm really *very* sorry," the stout woman said. "This isn't my office. It was the butler's, and since he left, I've been doing my best to mind things. I'm the cook," she added, in a gesture toward clarification.

"You certainly look as if you mind things very much," Gretsella said. She had never in her life seen such a flustered and harried-looking woman. Gretsella very rarely minded anything at all, and she was of the belief that her complexion had only benefited in consequence.

"Thank you very much, madam," said the visibly gratified cook. "I do my best. Did you want to talk about the dinner menus, madam?"

"I absolutely do *not*," Gretsella said. "I want to gossip. What's your name?"

"Prune, madam," Prune said. A wary look had crept across her face. "Amelia Prune. I'm never one to gossip, madam, especially about my betters. It's a very wicked thing to gossip, *especially* about one's betters, and I'm an honest, God-fearing woman."

Gretsella did her best to avoid a too-obvious wince. "But I'm not your better, Prune," she said. "I'm almost certainly your worse. And I came all the way down here for cake and gossip and will be *very* disappointed not to receive either."

Prune hesitated. A girl came in with cake and coffee, deposited the tray atop a pile of papers on the desk, and went out again.

Prune glanced around herself as if worried about spies, then leaned forward. "Who did you want to hear about, madam?"

"My son," Gretsella said. "What do the servants think of him? How has he been managing things? Who in the palace likes him, and who would like to see crows pecking his eyeballs out?"

"Oh, I'm sure that no one would ever think such a thing about His Majesty!" Prune said. "Although . . ."

"*Do* tell," Gretsella said. Then she whispered, "Is there someone at the door?"

Prune turned to look. Gretsella took the opportunity to sprinkle a little Powder of Volubility into her coffee. Prune turned back. "I don't hear anyone," she whispered.

"Oh, *wonderful*," Gretsella said, and picked up her own cup to take a very pointed sip. "Then we can have a lovely chat about people of our mutual acquaintance, as female friends who are absolutely not witches frequently do."

Prune looked somewhat stunned, which Gretsella took as evidence of her being very taken in by Gretsella's performance as a perfectly ordinary woman who would make an excellent confidante. "I, uh . . . yes, very nice," she said, and drank some coffee. Within a moment, her eyes had gone a little too bright. "You wanted to hear about how the new young king's been managing things, you said?" she asked, and then launched into a recital of Bradley's flaws so lengthy and detailed that Gretsella began to regret the strength of her own Powder of Volubility formulation. She did, at least, learn a great deal about the sheer extent to which Bradley's hand at the helm had immediately sunk the entire royal household into chaos. Many members of the staff who hadn't been fired for suspected loyalty to the previous king had quit shortly after Bradley's coronation, and the ones who'd stayed on were—as far as Gretsella could make out after sifting through all of Prune's editorializing—either too old to want to find a new position or too incompetent to look for one.

"That was the majordomo you saw out there, drunk as a lord shouldn't be," Prune said. "The only man worth an ounce of flour left around here is Old Herman in the stables."

"Ah, indeed," Gretsella said, and finished the last bite of her cake. It was chocolate cake, and very good. "This was a wonderful slice of cake, Mrs. Prune. Please give my compliments to the baker."

Prune looked extremely gratified to hear it. "But that's *my* recipe!"

Gretsella expressed surprise and delight. Prune expounded upon her joy. "What will my friends say when I tell them that the king's own mother likes my chocolate cake?!"

"There should be something to put up on the wall for that," Gretsella said. *That* might be a way for Bradley to improve his standing among the populace: by handing out little signs that said SUPPLIER OF FINEST CAKES TO THE KING or something like that. She would bring it up to Bradley. Or Janet, more likely. Janet would be the more practical choice. "You said something about a man in the stables?"

"Yes, madam, Old Herman," Prune said. She was beginning to get the droopy-eyed look that people took on when the Powder of Volubility started to wear off. "The stablemaster, madam."

"Thank you, Prune," Gretsella said. "You've been very helpful." Then she got up and left Prune there to slowly nod off into her cake.

Gretsella made her way down to the stableyard, which was located in a courtyard at the near center of the palace. *Near* center because the palace had no actual center: It was so wildly asymmetrical that, from above, it resembled a pancake made by a small child with a weak grip on the bowl of batter. The place had been the clear victim of centuries' worth of kings who'd been convinced that the architectural styles of previous eras were hideous and out of date, while the fashions of their *own* eras were clearly timeless and would easily withstand the scrutiny of future generations. The result was an ever-expanding architectural muddle, with each king's new additions and refurbishments patchily enveloping the modernization efforts of the previous three or four decades, like fungus overtaking a log. Among the infelicities were hallways that switched building materials and design styles halfway through before ending abruptly at blank walls; rooms with three round windows and one rectangular floor-to-ceiling window; and, in one notable instance in one of the two east wings, a turret stuck smack on top of another, larger turret. It was enough to drive a normal person into a state of absolute despair.

Gretsella liked it.

Whatever one thought of this baffling architectural compost heap, the stableyard was at the near center of it, and looked, mostly, like the stableyard that a sensible king might have built about eight hundred years ago—at least, that is, if one disregarded the sculptures of hideous fat cherubs that someone had added here and there above the doorframes. Gretsella disregarded them with extreme prejudice and marched into the stables to try to find someone who looked as if he might know what he was doing.

At first, she found just horses, which she could only assume were fine exemplars of their genus. Then she found a young man. "Excuse me," she said. "Could you direct me to Mr. Herman's office?"

"Ol' Herman? He's over there, ma'am," the young man said, and gestured toward a gray-haired man who was doing something very delicate-looking to the hoof of a horse.

Gretsella made her approach. "Hello, Mr. Herman. I am Gretsella, King Bradley's mother. I would like to speak to you."

"Just a tick, ma'am," Old Herman said, and spent a good minute or two finishing whatever he was doing—it smelled absolutely terrible, so Gretsella suspected the involvement of some sort of *wizard* potion—before setting the hoof down and straightening up. "How can I help you, ma'am? Are you looking for a nice, gentle gelding?"

"I would certainly prefer him over a *man*," Gretsella said, "but no. I'm looking for information."

Herman brushed his hands off on his overalls. He was a shortish, stoutish man with a round bald head, an enormous gray mustache, and very soft dark eyes. "All right," he said. "Cuppa coffee, then, ma'am?"

They went into a warm, tidy, hay-smelling office, and Herman brewed coffee over a little camp stove, then produced cookies from a battered tin with a picture of completely different cookies printed on it. "Now, then," he said, "what sort of information were you looking for, ma'am? If it isn't about horses, I don't know if I'll be able to help you much."

Gretsella found herself, in spite of her better instincts, liking him. She endeavored to rise above the sensation. "I'm trying to rebuild the palace staff," she said. "Currently, no one seems to be running the place at all. *Bradley* certainly isn't. I've been told that you're very sensible, so I've come to ask you who you think might be suitable in the role of housekeeper."

Herman nodded. "Well," he said, "that depends on whether you want someone who'll be loyal to the young king and do as he says, or someone who'll get the job done. Begging your pardon, ma'am."

"Don't beg my pardon," Gretsella said. "I'm looking for the latter. If they do what Bradley says, the palace will burn down within a fortnight." Then she added, "He's a very *nice* boy, really."

"That was my impression too, ma'am," Herman said. "Very . . . gentle. And kindhearted."

"He is," Gretsella agreed. "And affectionate. Like a dog. The kind with the long, soft ears."

"A spaniel," Herman said. "I think that's the kind you mean, ma'am. Very soft ears on a spaniel."

"*Possibly*," Gretsella said firmly. "On a subject unrelated to spaniels, *do* you know of anyone who might be a good palace housekeeper?"

"Well," Herman said, "if you want someone who understands palace business, then you might want to look for Lady Cordelia, ma'am. She was mistress of the robes to the old queen—that is, the *usurper's* wife, I mean, ma'am—and they ran her out when King Bradley came to power. She's not a political type, though. Just wants to do her job and keep things running smoothly. She'd be the one to speak to, ma'am."

"Thank you," Gretsella said. Then she asked: "I don't suppose, Mr. Herman, that you have a free afternoon once a week that you could dedicate to advising the king?"

CHAPTER 6

# In Which Gretsella Assembles Her Troops

Having left a highly astonished Herman in the stable-yard, an even more than usually smug Gretsella proceeded back to her room, where she was swiftly waylaid by a small, pink-cheeked, and crisply beaproned young girl. "Hello! I'm Trudy!" the girl said. "I'm your new lady's maid, ma'am."

Gretsella squinted at her. "Do you have much experience as a lady's maid, Trudy?"

"No, ma'am," Trudy said. "But I'll work very hard at it."

"I think you're supposed to curtsy," Gretsella said. "And witches don't *have* lady's maids. You can be my assistant instead."

Despite Gretsella's protestations, Trudy insisted on inserting herself into the process of Gretsella getting dressed, all the while peppering her with questions about what would be expected of her in her new role as a witch's assistant. Gretsella was tempted to tell her that maids shouldn't ask so many questions, but unfortunately, she had already said that Trudy could be her assistant, and there was nothing more important to a witch's success than being infuriatingly inquisitive whenever those around you would vastly prefer you to sit down and stop talking. Thus, as Gretsella's word was her bond (except when she was intentionally telling shocking falsehoods because it pleased her to do so), she set about giving Trudy a rudimentary introduction to the basics of witchery while Trudy vainly endeavored to put Gretsella's hair into a chignon. Unfortunately, some of Gretsella's curls had absorbed a bit too much magic over the years and now regarded hairpins as an invading force to be resisted with extreme prejudice. After Trudy nearly lost an eye for the second time, she gave up, grimly stuffed Gretsella's hair into a snood, and sent her on her way.

When Gretsella arrived in the great hall, it was already packed full of extremely jolly-looking merrymakers. This worked out nicely for Gretsella: Merrymaking made it easier for her to observe people from the shadows undetected. She lurked her way around the perimeter of the room, then advanced to the head of the table, where she accepted a kiss on the cheek from Bradley. "Hello, Mother," he said. "Won't you sit down and have something to eat?"

Gretsella sat down and had something to eat. Specifically, she had a small bit of every kind of sweet on the table, which resulted in a plate of food even bigger than the biceps on the knight who was currently making repulsive moon eyes at Bradley while talking loudly about all of his successful quests. Gretsella used some of the herb garnishes from a nearby platter of roast boar to curse him with watery bowels. Then she abandoned her station to turn herself invisible, creep around the room, and listen in on strangers' conversations, which was always her favorite part of any party.

# A Story About Listening

When Carrots was eighteen years old, she left her peaceful countryside home for the first time and struck out for the big city. In her younger, more innocent days of a year or two earlier, she had imagined herself doing this with only the clothes on her back and having a series of delightful adventures that ended in either an advantageous marriage or an exciting career on the stage. She was older now, though, and harder, and less full of faith in the truth of stories. She had also read a few novels that delicately hinted at the very bleak fate awaiting young women alone in the big city and at the mercy of its less-than-chivalrous male inhabitants. The details were left to the imagination, but Carrots's imagination had always been a powerful one. She decided that it might be a good idea to find a job first.

The job she found was as an oyster shucker in a little

restaurant owned by her aunt's best friend's sister-in-law. This was the sort of connection that was close enough to create a crushing sense of obligation but still distant enough to make venturing out of her little room and down into the shared kitchen almost painfully uncomfortable. Also uncomfortable was the job itself, which involved lots of salty ice water sloshing into the cuts that the rough shells made in her hands, even when she managed not to slice herself with her oyster knife. Still, she had the little room they'd given her and three free meals a day. Though her earnings were modest, they allowed her to spend her weekly half day off enjoying the big city the best way she knew how: by wandering the streets and watching other people.

There was a bit of an art to being a really good wanderer. One needed sturdy, sensible shoes, an umbrella in case of pouring rain or blazing sun, and comfortable clothes with a secret pocket for concealing money. One needed the ability to look, by turns, cold and hardened or fragile and innocent. One needed to be alert and attentive and very, very interested.

As Carrots discovered, she had this ability to feel interested in what the people around her were up to. It wasn't a bighearted, empathetic sort of interest. She wasn't listening in on the conversations of strangers so that she could sweep in like a fairy godmother and solve their problems. She was interested in people the way a bird-watcher was interested in birds, if the bird-watcher had at one point been treated with casual cruelty by a handsome young finch. She watched other people like a punter watched a Grand Guignol.

Her long walks around the city were ideal for observing people at large, for creating a personal catalog of all the types of humans she encountered: the roguish young man and the winking, red-nosed old man he would one day become; the chorus girl who came yawning out of her boardinghouse in the early afternoon; the drawn young mother selling flowers on the corner; the sober clerk hurrying home to his wife and children. Then, when she grew tired, she would find a place to examine her subjects more closely. One of these was at the little bar she'd found about three blocks from the oyster house. Tucked into a dark corner and halfway hidden behind a pillar was a little table where she could sit and listen in on other people's conversations.

She learned a lot from all of that listening. She listened to men who told the truth to their friends while drunk and then told outrageous lies to women while sober. She listened to girls who started out bright and optimistic but, as time passed, grew increasingly bitter and covetous. She listened to couples split up and get back together again. She listened to criminals discussing their crimes. She listened to it all and took careful note of everything.

After a while, she started to become familiar with individual characters, regulars like herself. She followed their lives as if they were plotlines in the serialized novels she used to enjoy in magazines. Sometimes, while she was shucking oysters, she'd daydream about what might happen to them next. Would Josie's young man finally propose? Would Old Mr. Gattersby finally be caught out as the source of all those bad pennies? Certain storylines presented themselves as more interesting than others. Then, very slowly and gradually, it occurred to Carrots that with all she'd learned about these people—and about people in general—it might be trivially easy for her to influence the courses of their lives in reality instead of just in her imagination.

She started off with what she thought would be a pair of particularly easy targets: a spinster named—unfortunately—Ermengarde Snip, and a poet several years her junior named Robert Crewe. Carrots had spent many long hours observing them both.

Miss Snip, an attractive-enough blond woman of forty or so, sometimes managed to claim Carrots's preferred corner when Carrots hadn't gotten there first. She liked to bring a book with her when she came, and often lingered for hours over a single glass of wine. At first glance, she might have been mistaken for a schoolteacher coming to the bar to pass a few inexpensive hours reading, but Carrots never stopped at the first glance. The wine Miss Snip sipped was the most expensive that the bar offered, her clothes were plain but made of fine material, and half the time, when she pretended to be reading her book, she was actually watching Mr. Crewe.

Mr. Crewe was about thirty, and had spent his entire youth writing poems that no one wanted to read. When he came to the bar, it was to scribble away furiously at his latest poem, to chat with the other young romantics who cluttered up the place, and to drink whatever someone else bought for him. What he lacked in talent, he made up for in having the dark hair and dreamy eyes that one expected from a poet, as well as a mind that thought high-minded concepts arranged into pleasant-sounding words were realer and truer than anything that had ever actually happened to him.

It didn't take much. Carrots started with Mr. Crewe, the easier target of the two. She began by expressing admiration for the (terrible) poem she'd just heard him recite to a long-suffering friend, then engaged him in more conversation about his *craft*—he was almost pathetically pleased to have his poems apparently taken seriously by a discerning reader—before segueing smoothly into the next phase of attack: telling him, more or less, the truth.

"I always think it's so interesting how when you live in the city, you might walk past a thousand people every day who have their own wonderful stories to tell that you'll likely never know about. So many people you see seem like such fascinating characters."

"Oh, you think so too?" Mr. Crewe asked, smiling at her. "I've always thought that *you* are a very interesting character. I've been noticing you hiding in that little corner, watching everyone and looking like the light of sunrise reflecting in the morning dew. I've always thought that you could be either a young forest witch or a milkmaid: just the pure fresh spirit of the countryside, in either case."

This was a moment when the whole trajectory of Carrots's life easily might have been set off in a different direction. It might have been such a moment for the even younger Carrots of just a few short years earlier. *That* Carrots might have still been willing to see herself as the protagonist, to see the sort of romance she'd once dreamed of spreading out in front of her. *This* Carrots, though, was different. She'd recast herself from leading lady to playwright, and didn't even notice the opportunity to take a starring role. Instead, she said, "Oh, not *me*. I'm extremely dull. I was thinking about Miss Snip."

"Miss Snip?" Mr. Crewe asked in the polite but detached tone of someone prepared to listen to a story about a person whom they neither knew nor cared about.

"Yes," Carrots said. "The slender lady with the sad blue eyes who always sits in that corner reading poetry. No, don't look!" she added at the end, which was, of course, exactly the thing to say to prompt Mr. Crewe to take a quick look. She saw him frown.

"Oh," he said. "I've seen her sitting there before, but I never took a closer look. I thought she was . . . well, she just looked like any old spinster in that old-fashioned dress with the high neck."

Something inside Carrots gave a little snarl at that. It didn't show on her face. Instead, she said, earnestly, "But she's not at all! I've been paying attention to her. I'm quite sure she was a real society beauty just a few years ago, but she must have had her heart broken by some scoundrel and never married. You can see her breeding in the quality of her dresses and hear it in her voice when she speaks, and you can tell by the books she reads, and by how attentively she listens whenever you recite your poetry, that she's a woman of real *sensibility*."

"I see," Mr. Crewe said, and turned his gaze toward Miss Snip. "Yes, I see. She does have a noble look about her, doesn't she? And even from this far away, you can still see the bright blue of her eyes."

In the sort of novel that Carrots read in those days, as a sophisticated young woman, Mr. Crewe's own eyes would harden and grow cold and calculating as he weighed this woman's worth. Instead, there at the bar, his gaze went soft and abstracted. He wasn't the kind of man who was capable of setting out to seduce a woman for her money. When he prepared himself to seduce this shy, lonely older lady, he did so thinking that he was acting with the heart of a poet recognizing a fellow traveler. And if there were other reasons lurking just beneath the level of conscious thought, did they matter in the moments when their eyes first met, when their hands first touched, when years later they sat together in the sitting room of their cozy, well-appointed country house and he read her poems he'd written for her that were filled with more sincere feeling than anything else he'd ever put to paper?

These weren't questions that entered Carrots's mind: neither during that conversation, when she prompted Mr. Crewe to look at his future wife for the first time, nor during any of the moments that followed, when she shepherded the two of them toward a union that caused a minor scandal in the more genteel neighborhoods of the capital. What she cared about was power—and the sheer, intoxicating, syrup-sweet joy of wielding it.

She slunk around the edges of the ballroom at their wedding, eavesdropping on other people's secrets and feeling a smug sense of self-satisfaction that was better, she thought, than anything she'd ever felt.

It was the first major manipulation of a long and fruitful career.

CHAPTER 7

# Back to the Feast Celebrating Gretsella's Arrival in the Capital

Most people at Gretsella's welcome feast were focusing on eating or flirting, oblivious to the fact that they were being invisibly monitored by the guest of honor. Janet was strumming her lute and not jesting even slightly. No one was overtly plotting to overthrow the king. One man was calling him a birdbrained fop, which Gretsella couldn't entirely disagree with. She dropped a spider into the man's soup anyway and then noticed whom he was speaking with: all hateful six or so feet of Sir Harold, wantonly flaunting his jawline with a buxom young woman on his knee. Gretsella dropped a lit candle down his tunic and, for a few moments, observed with great relish his hopping around and shrieking before she continued on toward the back of the hall.

She didn't find anything interesting until she got all the way to the back near the door, where a sad-looking man was skulking in the shadows like a witch at a wedding. He was holding a shield and wore a sword at his hip, and he looked as if he'd just come in out of the rain, but no one seemed to be taking the slightest notice of him. Gretsella re-visibilized herself. The knight—she assumed he must be a knight—barely jumped, which Gretsella found very annoying but also thought was to the fellow's credit.

"Hello, Grandmother," he said after a moment. "I beg your pardon. I didn't see you there."

"That's because I was *lurking invisibly,*" Gretsella said. She thought that she liked this knight. He had a smooth, dark complexion; his nails were neat and his braids tidy; and his voice was pleasant and low. Also, he was polite. If Gretsella was *forced* to speak to men, she preferred to speak to polite ones. "So that I could eavesdrop and drop a lit candle down Sir Harold's tunic."

"Oh," the knight said, and smiled, then quickly tried to pretend he wasn't smiling. "Why were you doing that, Grandmother?"

"He's been very inconsiderate to Bradley," Gretsella said. "And his jawline annoys me."

The knight, at the mention of Bradley's name, had gone a bit goggle-eyed. "You know King Bradley?"

"Yes," she said. "He's my son."

"*Oh,*" he said. "You must be so proud, Grandmother. He's such a lovely, kind"—he stopped and cleared his throat—"I mean, you must be very proud to be the mother of a king."

"Not particularly," she said. "There's nothing so very impressive about being a king. All you have to do is wait for your father to die, which happens to everyone, eventually. I was *much* prouder of Bradley when he was working as a hairdresser. Not everyone can cut hair like Bradley. It's an *art form*, you know." She felt, for a moment, as if she might sound a little ridiculous, but she swiftly drowned that thought in the deep bucket of her own self-confidence.

"I'm sure you're right, Grandmother," the knight said. "I certainly wouldn't trust myself to cut anyone's hair. They'd be lucky to come away with both ears still attached."

"You seem sensible," Gretsella said. "What's your name, and why are you all wet?"

"George," George said. "And I just arrived back. I've been riding for hours."

"And you came here instead of changing your clothes?" Gretsella asked, and watched as Sir George's eyes went straight to Bradley at the other end of the room before darting away again. "Ah. I see," Gretsella said.

Gretsella thought that Sir George looked uncomfortable, though she found it somewhat difficult to tell: Men very rarely looked comfortable in her presence. "I'd never presume, Grandmother. And, in any case, he'll never notice me."

"Oh, I don't know about that," Gretsella said, casting a critical eye over George's person. He was attractive enough, she supposed, as the menfolk went. He was also very neat and well-dressed, a characteristic that she often found greatly lacking in the men of her own village. The only point against him was what appeared to be a butter stain on his blue brocade vest. "Bradley struggles to completely ignore anything in trousers for longer than about five minutes."

George looked more uncomfortable than ever. "I think that he might be able to completely ignore me, Grandmother," he said, and then took a deep breath. "Just before I was born, my father evicted an old woman who lived in a cottage on his property."

"*Ah*," Gretsella said. "Did she turn up at your christening?"

"She did," said the gloomy Sir George. "My godmother had already gifted me with courage and strength in battle, so the old woman cursed me with never being noticed by anyone who mattered, and always turning up at any important function with a visible stain on my clothing."

Gretsella, despite her general admiration for a well-executed curse, couldn't help a sympathetic wince. "That would explain the butter on your vest, then."

Sir George didn't even bother to look down at himself to see. "Is it butter this time?" he asked. "Last time it was red wine. I don't even *drink* red wine."

"It's a very tidy little curse, if her goal was to keep you from cloaking yourself in glory," Gretsella said. "How does this not-being-noticed bit work? If I introduced you to Bradley, would he look right through you?"

"No," George said. "He just wouldn't take very much notice of me. With the old king, I had to be introduced to him three times before he could remember my name. The only thing that seems to make a difference is if I do something very valorous right in front of someone important and then get introduced to them a few minutes after, but even then, it's not a sure thing, really."

"Hmm," Gretsella said. "Interesting." Then she said, "Come with me, Sir George. I'm going to introduce you to someone."

If Sir George was disappointed when she led him directly to Janet, who was still strumming disconsolately on her lute, he didn't show it. He bowed to her very politely. Then Gretsella said, "Janet, I'd like you to write a nice song about Sir George."

Janet perked up a little as George began to look as if he'd just realized what a mistake he'd made. "What kind of song?"

"About the quest he was just on," Gretsella said. "Tell her, George."

George squirmed. "It was a very *juvenile* red dragon," he said.

"A *dragon*?" Janet asked, perking up even more. "Tell me all about it."

Gretsella left them to it and made her way back to the head of the table to sit next to Bradley, who was currently being flirted with by a maiden fair. Bradley was very politely fending her off, and seemed relieved to have a distraction when Janet began to sing a song.

*Brave, brave Sir George*
*Who always does his best,*
*Returned from slaying dragons now,*
*With butter on his vest!*

*A handsome knight, one must admit,*
*A hero bold and true,*
*His blood runs redder than the scales*
*Of the dragon that he slew!*

It wasn't, in Gretsella's opinion, a very good song, but she granted that it was better than she might have expected Janet to come up with on such short notice. George was hiding his face in his hands. Bradley was listening to the song with great evident interest. "Did one of my knights really slay a dragon?" he asked. "I don't think that we have a *Sir George* here, do we?"

"Of course you do," Gretsella said. "I was just speaking to him. I'll introduce him to you." Then, before Bradley could ask any more questions, she trotted over to where George was trying to blend into a tapestry of a boar hunt, grabbed him firmly by the elbow, and dragged him across the room to pay his respects to his king. This, at least, he did very nicely, with a graceful bow and a very reverent-sounding "Your Majesty" before he peeped up at Bradley through his long lashes.

Bradley was visibly interested. "Come sit by me," he said, "and tell me about your adventures, Sir George."

Sir George obeyed, and gave Gretsella a somewhat wild-eyed look as he sat down. Gretsella winked at him. Then she poured herself a glass of wine in honor of a job well done.

By the time she returned to her room, Gretsella was perhaps a bit less steady on her feet than her dearest friends and closest companions might normally expect, as well as significantly more cheerful than anyone who knew her would find right or natural. Her toadaphone was perched atop the bedpost. She cooed at it. "Hello, you lovely, warty thing! *Who's* a good toad? *You* are! A very good toad indeed!"

The toad took a deep breath, just like toads usually don't. Then it said, "All hail Bradley the Destroyer, who will bring about the end of the kingdom!"

Gretsella frowned. "Oh, *shut up*," she said. "Toads shouldn't *talk*." Then she put the toad into a hatbox, put the lid on the hatbox, put the hatbox out on the window ledge, and briskly slammed the window shut. "And *let that be a lesson to you*," she said. Then she went to bed.

The next morning, after an unrestful night of sleep in the too-soft feather bed, Gretsella retrieved her toad from the windowsill, ate a large bowl of pease porridge that she scooped for herself out of a vat intended for the palace staff, and headed off to look for Lady Cordelia, the former mistress of the robes.

She didn't find Lady Cordelia immediately. When she went to the address that Herman had provided for her, the servant girl told her that Lady Cordelia wasn't in.

"I see," Gretsella said. "I'll just wait here." Then she sat down directly on the steps.

The maid looked uncomfortable. "But you can't just sit *there*, madam."

"Oh, I assure you that I can," Gretsella said. "I'm very comfortable. I would be very sad to leave, really, when this is the coolest and smoothest step that I've ever had the pleasure of sitting on."

The maid hovered there for a moment, as if she were a

fruit fly and Gretsella an aging banana. Then she vanished back into the house. After a minute or so, she reappeared. "Lady Cordelia will see you now, madam."

"It's very kind of her to be so accommodating, considering that she isn't at home," Gretsella said. The maid shot her a look that strongly suggested she didn't find Gretsella *nearly* as full of wit and verve as Gretsella found herself. Then she led Gretsella inside.

Lady Cordelia was sitting in an armchair in her sitting room, working on a piece of embroidery that she set aside when Gretsella entered the room. She was, as far as Gretsella could see, a middle-aged woman of average height and weight, with hair neither short nor long and eyes neither dull nor piercing. For all that, she was a *lady*; the way she was dressed could really only be described with dismal adjectives like *sober* and *respectable*, words that Gretsella could proudly claim had never once been cast in her direction. In fact, Lady Cordelia's aura of extreme soberness and respectability was the only remarkable thing about her. If there were ever a hair out of place on Lady Cordelia, Gretsella assumed that the good lady would have it marched to the back of her head and shot as a warning to the other hairs.

Gretsella eyed Lady Cordelia. Lady Cordelia eyed her back. Cordelia was the first to crack. "Can I help you?"

"You can, in fact," Gretsella said. "I want you to work for my son. He needs a housekeeper."

Lady Cordelia raised her eyebrows, which were the kind of eyebrows that looked like they'd been clipped out of an eyebrow catalog and glued on. "I believe that you may have the wrong address," she said. "I am the daughter of a *baronet*."

"Congratulations," Gretsella said, "though I can't say that I consider being the relative of any *man* to be a particular accomplishment, speaking as the mother of a king."

They eyed each other some more.

"Which king is that?" Lady Cordelia finally asked.

"The current one," Gretsella said.

"Oh, *him*," Lady Cordelia said. "The one with the hair."

"That isn't the sort of tone most people around here take when talking about their king," Gretsella said. "But yes, the silly one with the hair, who right now is the only king that you've got."

"I feel as if I can take any tone that I like toward the man, considering the fact that it was I who stole away the orphaned prince and brought him to your doorstep about eighteen years ago," Lady Cordelia said. "Before I was the mistress of the robes, I was the young prince's nurse, and the closest the poor little nameless thing had to a mother. His christening was delayed by his mother's death, you know, so he had no name at all until you took him in. I knew that his great-uncle was fairly likely to have him killed, and I don't approve of the murder of babies. He was also very busily beheading any servants whom he suspected of having loyalty to his great-nephew, which I also thought ought to be stopped. I wrote several notes revealing Bradley's true identity and sent them to loyal friends both here and abroad. Then I told the former king that the young prince was to be raised as a commoner, knowing nothing of his true identity, but that if he didn't stop killing people and immediately give me a new position at court, the baby would be sent at once to Joymany to be raised with all titles and honors until the time came for him to reclaim his throne. I am socially acquainted with Lord Brigandale and had heard a tale or two from him about the troublesome local witch. I chose you to watch over the prince because I knew that a witch of Brigandale would have no foolish political entanglements of her own and thus would preserve a potential future king from forming any connections that would cause trouble for me if he did eventually reclaim the throne." She paused. "Also, it's very traditional to leave a royal infant to be raised by a witch. I like to respect the old ways, when practical."

The eyeing reached a fever pitch.

"Can you prove any of that?" Gretsella asked after a moment.

"Yes," Lady Cordelia said. "I have hidden away a lock of Bradley's hair, his receiving blanket, and a pressed rhododendron that I plucked from your garden on the day I left him on your doorstep next to the milk. Might I compliment you on your rhododendrons, by the way? I wouldn't be surprised to learn that they'd won several prizes."

This time, when they eyed each other, it was an eyeing of mutual understanding.

Lady Cordelia gestured toward an empty chair. "Won't you sit?"

Despite not being a witch herself, Lady Cordelia turned

out to be a hag of the highest order. The respectable blue-and-white sitting room rang out with the sound of their cackling. After they had successfully caricatured and resoundingly criticized every current member of Bradley's household staff, Gretsella returned the topic of their conversation to Cordelia's employment.

"We need someone *sensible* for the job, and you seem like the most sensible person I've met around here yet," Gretsella said. "It doesn't matter to me whether or not you think that Bradley should be king. I don't think he should be king either, but that doesn't mean I think the palace and the whole kingdom should be allowed to fall to pieces because poor Bradley isn't smart enough to figure out how to deal with them without having gone through any kind of apprenticeship program for kingdom management."

"You would think that if, as a society, we're to accept farm boys taking over all the complex levers of power that control the government upon the recommendation of a bunch of prophetic forest creatures, we would also institute some sort of civics training program for them to go through upon their arrival," Lady Cordelia said. "For *their* sakes as much as our own."

"Bradley is a hairdresser, not a farm boy," Gretsella said. "But I agree."

"You do?" Lady Cordelia asked. Then she recovered herself. "As you ought to, yes. What, exactly, would be the terms of my employment?"

Gretsella hadn't thought this part through yet, but she

didn't let that stop her from making wild pronouncements. "More generous than whatever they were in your last position," she said with enormous and unearned confidence. Considering what she knew about the state of the crown's finances, making such promises could be considered highly irresponsible. Fortunately for Gretsella, it wasn't in the tradition of witches to care about fiscal responsibility. She was sure that she'd figure something out. "Can you start work tomorrow afternoon?"

Lady Cordelia said that she could.

# Unnumbered Chapter from the Point of View of King Bradley, to Be Inserted Anywhere It Might Roughly Fit in with the Central Narrative

Bradley wasn't too stupid to know that he wasn't very smart.

He knew that people thought he had no idea that he didn't know very much. He never tried to prove them wrong. It made people uncomfortable to be around someone who was obviously dissatisfied with himself, and he always did his best to make people feel comfortable. Besides, it wasn't that he was *unhappy*, exactly. He tried to be a cheerful person. He just knew for a fact that some things were hard for him that other people seemed to be able to do without any difficulty at all.

When Bradley was a little boy, he'd sometimes gone with his mother to the mill to buy flour, and he'd watched the big millstone going around and around. The old stone was uneven, so you could see from the side that there were some spots where the wheat could sort of huddle down into a crack and the stone wouldn't be able to grind it into flour no matter what. That was what Bradley's brain felt like when he had to do something that wasn't very easy right away. Some things—like cutting hair or dancing or reading interesting novels—came to him almost instantly. Other things—like geography or cashing out at the salon at the end of the day—turned his brain into that millstone. He could feel the grinding. It wasn't a very nice feeling, so when he'd encountered it in the past, he'd usually turned toward the person nearest to him, given them his best smile, and explained that he thought they would do a much better job at solving his problem than he could. They usually did it right away, which fixed things temporarily, at least. It had never occurred to him that his strategy might fail him when something really important happened that he would have to deal with on his own.

Becoming king was a pretty important thing to have happened. The grinding had gotten so loud that it was hard to fall asleep at night.

On this particular morning, he'd slept especially badly and woken up feeling more tired than he ever had during his very brief career as a blacksmith's apprentice. As he shaved—he'd given up on being allowed to dress himself, but he drew the line at shaving, having been, after all, a *hairdresser*—he examined his face very carefully in the mirror. He didn't look *old*, exactly. He definitely looked *older.* That worried him. His face had worried him his whole life. People were always talking about it when they thought he couldn't hear them. *What a beautiful little boy*, they'd said, and now they said things like *What a gorgeous man.* Then they would smile at him. Sometimes they also said things like *You don't need brains with a face like that!*, which was exactly what worried him. He didn't need brains with a face like this, but he knew that one day he'd wake up with a face that called for a little more brain than he'd been given. He knew this because he'd been told so, spitefully, by his best friend in elementary school, a little girl named Gillie who had dramatically ended and then reaffirmed their friendship at least twice a month. He'd gone to his mother about it in tears. "Mother," he said, "Gillie says that I'm going to get old and ugly one day and everyone will hate me because I'm so stupid!"

"Don't be ridiculous," his mother had said. "People won't hate you. You're a very nice boy, and you'll stay that way when you're old and wrinkled and have hair growing out of your nose."

That hadn't comforted him back then. It didn't comfort him now either. He was fairly sure that what from a handsome young man was charming grew very quickly intolerable when it came with lots of hair growing out of his nose.

In any case, his worry about his face was, in a way, what had gotten him out of bed despite his exhaustion this morning, just as it had almost every morning since he'd become king. He was trying to educate himself. He'd had one of his knights buy a lot of very important, difficult books for learning about things like ethics and astronomy and law and foreign languages and other things that a king should know, and he studied them for two hours every morning before the lords of the robes et cetera came marching in to pull on his socks.

This morning, he was attempting to learn about macroeconomics. His brain ground more loudly than it ever had, he was sure, in his entire life.

There was a knock on the door.

"Come in," Bradley said. Then he changed it to "Enter!" because that sounded more kingly.

The knocker entered. It was Sir George. Bradley immediately started blushing. George gave a very elegant bow. "Your Majesty," he said, "I saw the light under the door as I passed, and I thought that I might invite you to join me for a ride. It's more pleasant in the morning, before it gets too hot." It was early enough in the day that it still wasn't completely light out.

George, Bradley thought with a surge of despondency, probably knew all about macroeconomics. He probably did seven brisk macroeconomics every morning after his coffee and before his push-ups. "That's very kind of you, Sir George, but I'm afraid that I have work to do," Bradley said, politely. Not that he'd consciously decided to speak politely: That was just the only way he knew how to talk. George's eyes flicked down to the books on the desk. Bradley blushed harder. He tried to cover the books with a casual arm but instead sent them all cascading to the floor in an agonizingly prolonged chorus of rustles and thumps.

George rushed to help him pick them up, because that was the sort of person George was. He was a picker-up of things that other people had knocked over. When he saw what he was picking up, he said, in his warm, quiet way, "Oh, you're studying economics, Your Majesty? I don't think I'd be able to manage that this early in the morning. When I was in school, I remember thinking it was interesting in the sort of way that made your head ache after about an hour."

"It's not so bad," Bradley said. "A little difficult." George was looking at him kindly. Bradley blurted out, "I think that I'm too slow to understand it." Then he felt himself go tense. He knew better than to say that sort of thing. There was just something about George that shook the honesty out of him like sauce out of a bottle.

There were certain faces that people usually made at Bradley when he'd said things like that, back before he'd learned not to. There was the quickly-covered-up sneer of disgust. There was the exaggeratedly furrowed brow and downturned lips of pity. There was the bared-tooth rictus of extreme discomfort. George didn't make any of those faces. He looked at Bradley very calmly and said, "I don't think that you are, Your Majesty."

Bradley squirmed, his heart sinking. This was, possibly, the worst reaction of all: when people looked at his handsome face and assigned brilliance to him that he simply didn't possess. "I'm not being modest," he said. "I've been reading this for hours, and I still can't make any sense of it."

George gave a thoughtful nod. "I don't mean to argue with you. You know better than anyone how quick or slow you are. But I think that most people who really understand this sort of thing took more than an hour or two to get there." He paused. "If you like, Your Majesty, maybe you could tell me where you're having difficulties, and I could try to help. Sometimes I won't understand something that I read in a book, but it all comes clear when someone explains it to me."

"Oh," Bradley said. He flushed. "Well . . . I always used to hear people complaining about taxes. Talking about how the nobility was robbing them blind and they couldn't afford to feed their children—things like that. So the first thing I did when I became king was cancel all of the taxes, and then everyone started talking about how I'd ruined the economy, and how there were starving people filling the public squares because of me." He swallowed. "I only wanted to help, but it all went wrong, and all of my advisers sigh or smirk or lie to me and tell me that the people are just ungrateful when I try to ask questions about it. So I tried reading these books, but they don't say anything at all about what happens when you cancel all of the taxes."

"That might be because no one has done it before exactly the way you did," George said. "But I think that the trouble with all of this economics stuff is that anything you do can have all sorts of different effects that you didn't plan on. Like, have you ever heard of a holly dragon, Your Majesty? Where I grew up, we used to nail them over the doorframes to guard our homes on Midwinter's Night."

"Oh, of course," Bradley said. "I think they must have them everywhere in Evermore. I loved putting ours up every year."

"And did you ever try to buy one on Midwinter's Day?"

Bradley shook his head hard. "We always had one for free. Mother grows holly in the garden and makes her own. She always said that she'd burn herself at the stake before she'd pay what they sell them for at the shops, especially just before Midwinter."

"Your mother is a very intelligent woman," George said with the exact sort of expression on his face that people usually had when they complimented Bradley's mother. "Why are holly dragons so expensive?"

"Because everyone needs a holly dragon to guard the door at midnight," Bradley said. "So the shops can set whatever price they like, especially just before Midwinter, when the stocks are running low."

"Exactly," George said. "A holly dragon is indispensable. People will pay any price to get one. And around that time, all of the servants and clerks and apprentices have gotten their Midwinter bonus, so they have more cash to spare and might be willing to spend a little extra on the last holly dragon in town. That's one of the things that happened when you canceled the taxes, Your Majesty. Everyone had a bit more cash in their pockets than they usually did, so they rushed out to buy things that they usually wouldn't. Then there weren't enough of the things that they wanted—like holly dragons—to go around, so the merchants raised their prices. When it happens across a whole country, they call it inflation, and it can cause problems when it happens very quickly. Then there was the drought at the same time, of course, which meant there was less grain to make into bread, which made everything worse."

"Oh," Bradley said, and grabbed one of the books he'd been looking at to hunt down the chapter that had talked about inflation. He stared down at the page. It was almost as incomprehensible as before, but now, at least, there was a word in it that he could understand. "It makes sense when *you* explain it."

"You explained it to yourself," George said. "I just helped. You needed something you could picture in your head, that's all, instead of a bunch of dry academic abstractions."

"The holly dragon," Bradley said. "I understood the holly dragon." His face was getting warm again. "Thank you, George."

George inclined his head. It wasn't quite a bow. "You're welcome, Your Majesty."

Bradley licked his lip. "Please call me Bradley."

"Bradley," George repeated, and looked him in the eye. Bradley's face grew hotter.

In the rafters above them, a small gray mouse gave a nod of approval.

# A Digression on the Subject of Fairness, and the Lack Thereof

Once upon a time, about fifty years ago, Gretsella—the witch of Brigandale, who was just starting out in the witchcraft industry and hadn't yet settled on reasonable prices as her unique selling proposition—moved into a cottage not very far away from her mother's. This, it turned out, was a mistake.

She'd tried her luck in the capital, but it hadn't worked out. The rents were wildly unreasonable, and there were too many other established witches around for a young aspiring witch to really get a toehold in the industry. So she'd moved back home to Brigandale, a decision she quickly started to regret.

Her mother was the problem. She refused to take Gretsella seriously, even if she kept insisting that she *did, of course I take you seriously, Greta*. She kept calling Gretsella *Greta*, despite Gretsella reminding her over and over again that *it's Gretsella now, Mother.* Greta was the name that her mother had given her, after her grandmother. *She was such a wonderful woman,* Gretsella's mother would say. *When you were a baby, I used to cry, sometimes, thinking about how unfair it was that she never got to meet you.* The first Greta had been a wonderful woman, Gretsella was told, because she was gentle, and kind, and made the best pies in the world, and was adored by children and animals. These were not the ways in which Gretsella wanted to be wonderful. She didn't want to be another nice little Greta having a nice little life in the cottage down the way. She'd told her mother that a *hundred* times, but her mother kept calling her Greta half the time anyway, and claiming that it had been an accident. Gretsella's mother also kept doing things like asking her when she thought she might get married, and whenever Gretsella would remind her mother that she had a career as a witch, her mother would say something like *I don't see why a witch can't find a nice man to settle down with,* and Gretsella would snap at her mother, who would leave Gretsella's cottage in tears, as if she hadn't started the whole argument in the first place.

It was all so infuriating that Gretsella would sometimes refuse to speak to her mother for months on end, until eventually she'd give in and drop by her mother's house with the excuse that she needed to borrow a few eggs or wanted her apple cake recipe so she'd have something to bring to the next meeting of her coven. It was on one of these occasions that Gretsella walked into her mother's kitchen, got a good look at her mother's face, and knew immediately that something was very, very wrong.

Once upon a time, in the Great Forest of Brigandale in the magical Kingdom of Evermore, a young witch found out that her mother was dying of cancer, and there wasn't a thing she could do about it. In every time and every place, there are some things that even magic can't do much to change.

Gretsella's mother died only a few weeks after that. No one ever called her Greta again.

About thirty years after the day of her mother's funeral, Gretsella held a wriggling baby boy in her arms, pressed her nose into his soft black hair, and said, *It isn't fair, Bradley. It isn't fair, it isn't fair, it isn't fair.* Her shoulders shook, and her voice cracked, but there was no one there to say if her eyes were red and puffy later that day, or if her voice was raspy, or if she struggled to get through her evening's chores. By that time, she had spent thirty years without anyone who would notice or care about her tears.

CHAPTER 7.5

# In Which Gretsella Enlists the Help of a Villain

After they'd shaken hands to establish the beginning of Lady Cordelia's new career, Gretsella asked another question. "Since you're so sensible," she said, "you might be able to help me with another little problem. Do you know anyone who might be able to get the Treasury into order? I suspect that the last person to chew through the palace accounts was a rat."

"The last man employed to chew through them was a rat as well," Lady Cordelia said. "Mr. Kedge. He was the master of the Treasury before your son took over. A very clever fellow. Good at his job."

"And where is he now?" Gretsella asked. "He hasn't left town, I hope?"

"That would be very unlikely," Lady Cordelia said. "The last I heard, he was in the palace dungeon."

Gretsella blinked. "Why? What did he do?"

"Ask your son," Lady Cordelia said. "He's the one who put him there."

"I think I'll do that," Gretsella said, and then said her goodbyes, though not before extracting a promise from Lady Cordelia that she would attend a meeting at the palace the following afternoon.

Gretsella headed straight back to the palace and from there set out to locate her son. He wasn't in the great hall, nor was he in his kingly bedchamber. Gretsella cast a Spell of Location and followed the loud, irritating clanging sounds to the stableyard, where she found two fully armored men mounted on horses and galloping at each other at top speed. Gretsella couldn't help but feel a grudging sense of respect for the sheer level of almost witchly dedication to noise, chaos, and the heady potential of technically-accidental-yet-surely-inevitable maiming that was being exhibited before her. "Stop that right now!" she called out after she'd spent a few minutes watching them with the sort of mingled disgust and fascination that she normally reserved for the sight of an owl hacking up a pellet.

The armored knights didn't stop, possibly because they couldn't hear her through the soup tureens they were wearing on their heads. Gretsella directed her attention to the horses. "Stop running back and forth like that *this instant*," she said. "You look completely ridiculous."

The horses stopped running, looking frankly relieved that someone had finally pointed out the obvious and allowed them to give up on this whole pointless endeavor. One of them started snuffling at a small patch of grass that had somehow survived all of the galloping.

The two mounted personages did a bit of light spurring and gee-upping, trying to encourage their horses back into motion. The horses placidly ignored these attempts. Eventually, the closest knight spotted Gretsella. "Oh, Mother," he said, and opened up his visor, revealing the familiar handsome face and baffled expression of her only son. "Why couldn't you have just asked us to stop?"

"I tried," she said. "You couldn't hear me. And I have to speak to you about something."

Sir George—he was, of course, the other rider—had by this point dismounted and led his horse over by the reins to see what was going on. Gretsella eyed him consideringly. She hadn't specifically *told* the horse not to be *led*, but horses usually took a broad interpretation of her instructions. Either this horse was particularly fond of its master, or Sir George was a rare example of a man who'd been so thoroughly witch-cursed as a child that some of the witchiness had stuck to him.

"What did you want to speak to me about?" Bradley asked, dismounting as well so that he could speak to her as politely as possible.

"The accountant in your dungeon," Gretsella said.

Bradley blinked. "There's an accountant in my dungeon?"

Sir George cleared his throat. "Mr. Kedge, Your Majesty. The former master of the Treasury. You had him imprisoned for thieving from the crown."

"*Oh,*" Bradley said. "*That* accountant. What do you want with him, Mother?"

"To give him a job, probably," Gretsella said. "I think that the palace accounts are currently being overseen by a flock of pigeons."

Sir George recoiled. "You'd give Kedge a job? But the man is dishonorable!"

"Which is exactly what you'd want from a man who's managing your money," Gretsella said.

Bradley was looking between the two of them with a distinctly anxious air. "Well, I don't really know—"

"Just haul him out of the dungeon, Bradley," Gretsella said. "Give him an opportunity to explain himself. If you don't remember him, you couldn't possibly have spoken to him in person. Giving him another chance would be a very kind and just and kingly sort of thing to do."

Bradley looked relieved. "You're right," he said. "A good king *should* always try to be just." Sir George didn't say anything—he wouldn't, Gretsella assumed, want to contradict his king—but she noticed him eyeing her with something like respect for a worthy opponent. She winked at him. He ducked his head and tried to hide his smile with his hand.

As much as she could ever like a man who wore a soup tureen on his head, Gretsella had to admit that she didn't mind Sir George.

Bradley, with his usual courteousness, begged his mother to give him and Sir George some time to get out of their armor and generally refresh themselves. Gretsella just as courteously agreed, on the basis that they both smelled too awful to be spoken to indoors, and passed the ensuing hour or so prowling around the east wing of the palace, opening any doors that looked interesting and acting as if anyone who expressed any discomfort over having just been walked in on during a private moment was the one who was being strange and unreasonable.

Eventually, they all met again in the antechamber outside Bradley's bedroom, where the king was accustomed to receiving his guests. Said guests were received at an enormous golden desk that made Bradley look depressingly like an actual puppet king when he perched himself on the large velvet-upholstered chair behind it. After a few minutes, two palace guards—one of them still appearing distinctly parroty around the beak area—marched in holding a surprisingly young man between them. This was, presumably, the dishonorable Mr. Kedge. He was small, blond, and wearing a rumpled and faded old black suit, like the village undertaker if the undertaker had recently been chased down a very steep hill. There was a strangely fervent gleam in his little blue eyes. There was a similar gleam in the former parrot's eyes, though this was directed straight at Gretsella. She accepted his hatred as her due.

"Your Majesty," Mr. Kedge said, and attempted an elaborate bow that was arrested by the guards who were still gripping his arms.

"Mr. Kedge," Bradley said, and half stood out of instinctual politeness before remembering that kings weren't supposed to do that and sitting down again, looking exhausted by his current circumstances. "Uh, sit down, please?" Then, apologetically to the guards: "You'll have to let go of his arms."

The guards released him, and Mr. Kedge stumbled forward. He managed to land heavily in a large gilt chair that made him look even more like a dirty little boy at a funeral. "I await your pleasure, Your Majesty," he said breathlessly.

Bradley looked embarrassed at having encountered someone who was even more elaborately polite than he was. "You used to be the master of the Treasury?"

Mr. Kedge leaned forward in his chair. "I was the master of the Treasury in name, Your Majesty," he said. "And if you forgive me, Your Majesty, I remain so in spirit!"

". . . *Oh*," Bradley said.

It seemed clear to Gretsella, at this juncture, that she would have to take things further into hand if she wanted anything at all accomplished. She grabbed one of the gilt chairs and dragged it around to Bradley's side of the table with a satisfying screeching, scraping sound. Then she sat down next to Bradley, leaned across the table toward Mr. Kedge, and said, "If you take your job so seriously, how did you end up thrown in a dungeon for embezzling from the crown?"

Mr. Kedge leaned even farther toward her in response, to the point that he seemed in imminent danger of toppling forward and braining himself on the edge of the desk. The blue eyes gleamed with certainty. "But I *was* doing my job, madam! I only ever did as I was asked by His Majesty, the former king, madam, and he asked to have a percentage of funds received from the crown's properties in the southern valleys sent to his bankers in Borgravia every quarter while not making this clearly evident in the accounts, madam! I would never dream of questioning His Majesty as to *why* he wanted me to manage the numbers as he did. My only role was to *manage* them. And I *did* manage them! In their many thousands, madam! In all of their logic and certainty, in all of their golden, clinking virtue, I managed them! In all of their tidy columns, madam, and their every elegant row!"

". . . *Oh*," Gretsella said.

There was a moment of silence as she considered what she ought to do with this clearly dangerously insane individual. Mr. Kedge smiled gently back at her. She cleared her throat. "Would you manage them for anyone? And into any configuration? And figure out where the money was going if it seemed to be wandering off on its own, for example?"

"I *would*, madam," he said, and then paused. "If I was provided with a salary. And my own suite of rooms. And a chain of office. The master of the Treasury is *always* given a chain of office."

"A *nominal* salary," Gretsella countered. "Since you'd be . . . on probation. But with the suite of rooms and chain of office." The palace was full of empty rooms that they could use to house one small, strange man, and she was sure that they could dig up a chain out of a cupboard somewhere. Mr. Kedge looked as if he was considering her offer. She added, "And a special hat."

Mr. Kedge visibly brightened. "A hat, madam?"

"A hat," Gretsella confirmed. "A distinctive hat. So that

when you walk down the street, people will say, 'There goes the master of the Treasury in his extremely distinctive hat that only he is allowed to wear, upon penalty of death!'"

"Mother—" Bradley began.

Gretsella ignored him. "What do you say to that, Mr. Kedge?"

"I'd agree to it with a joyous heart, madam!" said Mr. Kedge, and they shook on it then and there.

"You can report to work tomorrow morning," Gretsella said, "and be assigned your rooms. Once you've performed satisfactorily for a week, you can have the chain and the hat. If you don't show up to work tomorrow, I'll turn you into a chicken and have you put on exhibit at county fairs—you'll be solving arithmetic problems with your beak."

Mr. Kedge paled slightly at this threat and swore he would appear at the appointed time. Then he very swiftly walked backward, away from Bradley, until he could dart out of the room.

"Mother," Bradley said once the accountant was safely out of earshot, "do you really think it's wise to hire him back? He did commit crimes, after all."

"He committed crimes *for his former employer*," Gretsella said. "That's exactly the sort of person you want handling your money. Perfectly honest with you, and perfectly dishonest with everyone else."

"I suppose there must be something to that," Bradley said after a long moment. "Like with lawyers." He still had his face all creased up: It usually did that when he was venturing into the uncharted waters of forming an independent thought.

"Exactly," Gretsella said. Then she waved over the guards. "You two! Do you only drag people here against their wills, or can you send messages as well?"

The guards conceded that they were capable of carrying a message, though the still-somewhat-parrotified fellow didn't look pleased about it.

"Good," Gretsella said. "I want you to tell a few people to come here tomorrow morning for an audience with the king."

The guards did as they were told, if reluctantly, and the next morning, Gretsella found herself proudly presiding over a fine assemblage of various useful personages. There was Lady Cordelia, looking crisp and tidy and gratifyingly witch-like in highly starched black. There was Janet: alert, attentive, and drinking too much coffee. Next to her sat Sir George, who only had eyes for Bradley, and beyond him Mr. Kedge, even more alert than Janet despite politely declining a cup of coffee on the grounds that he took "no strong drink of any kind." Then, finally, there was Herman, who mostly looked puzzled over having been invited.

Gretsella outlined her plans to them. She couldn't give any of them noble titles, but she could give them jobs. Some of their roles were obvious. Lady Cordelia would be taking over the role of housekeeper, tasked with keeping the palace running and the servants mostly propped up on both feet. Mr. Kedge would be responsible for getting the accounts into order and working with Lady Cordelia to identify where the palace could best economize. The others, however, were given roles that she knew they hadn't expected.

"Janet," she said, "the king has decided to assign you the position of Chief Jester and Minister of Propaganda." Then she gave Bradley a quick warning kick under the table to let him know that his decisions were final, even when he'd only just now been informed that he'd made them.

Janet looked pleased, then confused, then pleased again. "Oh," she said. "I'm sure that I'll do my best to fulfil His Majesty's expectations, Grandmother." Then she ventured: "What exactly is a minister of propaganda?"

"They're all the rage in Overthere," Gretsella said. "And other Abroad places." She'd learned all about them from one of the newspapers that she didn't read. "Their job is to convince the people that they're all wildly lucky to live where they live, and that the king is the best king who ever could have reigned, and that they definitely don't want to violently overthrow anybody."

Janet sat up even straighter in her chair. She was the sort of educated young person who was always very impressed by things that they did Abroad. "That sounds like an interesting job," she said. "Convince them with songs and jesting, you mean? Can I have a budget? The quickest way to get people to listen to what we want them to hear would be to have other people singing the songs I write, and the fastest way to do that would be to get sheet music printed and distributed for free in bars. People will like anything if they hear it often enough, and musicians will play anything if they don't have to pay for it."

"Very clever," Gretsella said. "I knew that I could count on you. Find her some money, Mr. Kedge."

Mr. Kedge said that he would, though he used so many impassioned words to do so that Lady Cordelia looked as if she regretted having agreed to work with him. Next, Gretsella turned her attention toward Sir George, who was valiantly attempting to adjust his left sleeve to hide the prominent stain on its cuff. Tomato sauce, Gretsella thought. At least it would be easier than the butter stain to scrub out. "Sir George," she said, "I'd like you to serve as the king's personal secretary. You know, writing his letters, arranging his calendar, making sure that he gets out of bed at the right time in the morning, giving sage advice when he asks for it. That sort of thing."

"*Oh* . . ." Sir George said. The phrase *gets out of bed* had induced him and Bradley to simultaneously develop some sort of terrible disorder that caused their eyes to dart all over the room and land absolutely everywhere but on the face of the other person currently under discussion. "It's a very great honor, madam. Thank you."

"You're very welcome," Gretsella said generously. She liked Sir George, and she particularly liked that he served as an excellent distraction from men whom she liked much, much less. The more time George spent hanging around Bradley, the fewer the opportunities Bradley would have to get distracted, wander off, and fall into a sticky pit full of strong forearms and dubious motivations.

From the other side of the table, Herman cleared his throat. "Pardon me," he said, "and meaning no disrespect, but what am I doing here? I doubt you need a Chief Minister of Stables."

"I don't care about stables," Gretsella said. It was important to not allow the menfolk to come to the mistaken impression that you cared about the things that interested them. "Everyone here is on Bradley's advisory council now. Your job is to be sensible and tell him when he's being silly if I'm too busy to tell him first. You will be Chief Minister of Good Sense and Practicality."

"Begging your pardon again, ma'am," Herman said, "but I don't think that calling a king silly would be very good for my health."

"Don't worry about that," Gretsella said immediately. "Bradley is much too gentle and just and true a king to have anyone's head chopped off for giving him a bit of constructive feedback on his work performance. Isn't that right, Bradley?"

Bradley looked exactly as confused as usual, but significantly more shocked and appalled. "I don't want to chop *anyone's* head off!"

"You see!" Gretsella said, and then clapped her hands. "Excellent. Off you all go. Time to get to work!"

Everyone, including Bradley, glanced nervously at one another. Sir George cleared his throat. "Your Majesty," he murmured, "may we all be dismissed?"

"Oh! Right. Yes, go ahead and leave, everyone," Bradley said. Everyone darted to obey. Except Gretsella, of course. She didn't have any reason to stay, but it was against her firmly held spiritual beliefs to gratify other people's politely worded requests in a timely fashion. "Not you, Sir George," Bradley said quickly. "I need you to . . . do personal secretary things. Immediately."

"Oh," Sir George said. "Of course, Your Majesty."

The two of them were looking at each other with absolutely revolting expressions of mutual fondness and admiration. "*Ugh,*" Gretsella said, very loudly and disruptively. Then she left to go find some cake.

CHAPTER 8

# In Which Gretsella's Efforts Achieve Results

Predictably, time passed. Just as predictably, Gretsella was proved right. Everything functioned much better when sensible, responsible people were in charge. After a few months, the palace's affairs were running along as smoothly as the buses on the public highways weren't. Mr. Kedge had whispered into the ears of his beloved numbers sweetly and tenderly enough to have discovered all sorts of areas where the palace could economize, all of which were swiftly acted upon by the formidable Lady Cordelia. He'd also convinced Bradley to levy high taxes on certain products used primarily by the wealthy, like fur capes and little silver forks that were only used to eat sardines. The income from these new taxes on luxury goods was then used to shore up holes in the budget, obviating the need to send knights out into the countryside to rip the silver buttons off the coats of the few remaining peasants who could still afford buttons in this economy, to say nothing of the coats.

Within the palace itself, Lady Cordelia had fired a number of people, hired several more, and ruthlessly imposed order upon the newly scrubbed and starched foot soldiers in her domestic army. The kitchen was cleaned top to bottom, hygiene practices were instituted for the kitchen maids, and fashionable new menus were forced upon the head cook. Rooms that had been locked up and empty for years were opened, scoured, refurbished, and prepared for visitors. A variety of guests had been invited to attend the series of balls and tourneys organized by Lady Cordelia to formally present King Bradley to the noble families of Evermore and the kingdom's allied nations. She and Sir George had also created a daily schedule for Bradley to follow, with set times for him to grant audiences to his increasingly devoted and appreciative subjects.

While all of this was going on in the palace, Janet had been going out among the people, spreading pro-Bradley propaganda wherever she went. One particular song that managed to be both humorous and complimentary about Bradley's good looks had become a music hall sensation, and Gretsella often heard it being sung very loudly and horribly in taverns when she slunk around the city at night. (She liked to slink around the city at night in pursuit of such wicked business as peeping through windows to see how strangers liked to decorate their living rooms and cutting interesting long-stemmed flowers out of other people's gardens to use in her floral arrangements.) A more straightforward song of praise had been taken up by many of Bradley's most fervent admirers to be sung whenever he appeared on a balcony to wave to the adoring masses gathered below.

Any ordinary citizen of Evermore would be excused for thinking that their young, handsome, fortunate king was delighted with his lot in life. They would, therefore, be surprised and baffled to be presented with the morose and wan face of King Bradley as it appeared over breakfast, or between audiences with various vassals, or as he shuffled through the palace halls with his fur-lined cape dragging along behind him like the tail of a dispirited border collie.

At first, Gretsella ignored this behavior. She let him stew. *He* was the one who had decided that it would be a good idea to flirt and right-hook his way into being responsible for the well-being of the nation: He could spend a few days reflecting on how deeply misguided that decision had truly been. She waited like a snake watching a particularly fat chipmunk, monitoring the dolefulness of his window-out-gazing and the gustiness of his sighs.

All of this reign-induced misery made Bradley somewhat offensive as a companion, so Gretsella spent her time in the much more congenial company of Old Mr. Herman in the stables, who served her tea and cookies and managed to maintain his good sense and cheerful demeanor even in the face of her most irritating behavior. She found this invigorating in the way that she imagined cats must enjoy encountering particularly spirited mice.

One morning, Gretsella woke up in her luxurious dowager

suite and had the thought that there was really no point living in a palace where a fleet of servants catered to your every whim unless you had someone to show off to. With this in mind, she enchanted the mirror in her bedroom—it was truly extraordinary how well they worked when they weren't *sulking*—and called a convocation for the following Sunday.

The members of Gretsella's coven agreed to be treated to lunch at the palace with an alacrity that spoke only ill of their characters, the wretched, grasping bunch of social-climbing witches that they were. Gretsella had expected no less. They all arrived very promptly, each dressed in a fashion that they thought suited the occasion. Hyssop and Yarrow each wore their finest black silk robes and pointed hats, with discreet little decorative brooches on their chests, Hyssop's a silver bat with rubies for eyes and Yarrow's a cat with eyes made of emeralds. Magnetia also arrived in traditional black, but she had ornamented her ensemble with a bewildering array of buckles and pins that didn't seem to perform any discernible function in terms of connecting or fastening, in addition to an enormous number of brooches, rings, and necklaces similar in design to those worn by Yarrow and Hyssop but of obviously much lower quality. Barb, for her part, was wearing a black linen sundress and a pointy black straw hat. She had accessorized with a charm bracelet from which dangled tiny cats, broomsticks, cauldrons, et cetera, and she carried a matching black straw bag. She looked very nice, which was extremely annoying of her.

Sartorial matters aside, the convocation was a great success. Bradley was extremely supportive—*It's so nice that you've invited your friends over, Mother*—and stopped by with Sir George to say hello halfway through their luncheon, which precipitated an amount of giggling and cooing and cackling that Gretsella found frankly unbecoming from a group of accomplished hags. He also instructed Janet to give the witches a thorough tour of the palace and grounds, with all appropriate attention to be paid to relevant and entertaining historical anecdotes et cetera. Janet did an admirable job, though she seemed a bit self-conscious to be in the company of so many witches when she herself was neck-deep in denial of her true nature. Hyssop, Yarrow, and Barb kept giving each other knowing glances and then smiling at Janet so condescendingly that you could practically hear the clumps of precipitated smugness hitting the floor. Janet and Magnetia, meanwhile, kept stealing furtive little glances at each other. Eventually, just after relating an amusing story about a gargoyle that was said to be the petrified familiar of an ancient warlock, Janet burst out with "I just wanted to say that I totally love your outfit!"

"Oh my Go—devil, thank you!" Magnetia trilled. "It's all thrifted!"

This set off a degree of witchly shrieking and burbling between the two of them that would have chilled the bones of the doughtiest of priests or clerics. The elder witches eyed one another, then shrugged collectively. The youth had their ways, no doubt. It was nice to see two junior witches bonding, even if it was over paying real currency to buy someone else's smelly old clothes.

After this highly successful social event came to an end, Gretsella had nothing else left to occupy her other than monitoring her son, which she rededicated herself to with renewed energy and zeal. Finally, after what Gretsella felt was a suitably lengthy exposure to subtle psychological warfare, Bradley sighed so loudly over lunch that the startled footman jumped and spilled the gravy, and Gretsella decided that her son was ripe for a nice old-fashioned motherly manipulation. "Bradley, my dear," she said, and then immediately regretted it. She never called him "my dear." She had noticed in Bradley, as of late, an increasing and slightly alarming predisposition toward forming *thoughts* and, from those thoughts, *conclusions*. He might become suspicious. She coughed and pounded her fist against her chest for a moment in an attempt to give the impression that the "my dear" had been brought on by a passing spasm in her lungs. Then she started over. "Bradley," she said, "what's troubling you?"

"Oh, Mother," he said, and started pouring his heart out all over the lunch table. Gretsella found this somewhat inconsiderate of him, considering the fact that the table had already been soiled by almost an entire boatful of gravy, but she made sympathetic sounds in her throat and patted his hand as he talked. There were, it seemed, a number of things troubling Good King Bradley. Some of his knights, annoyed with him for his decision to tax fine furs and sardine forks and fancy gold-plated jousting outfits instead of boring things like bread, had been behaving as frostily toward him as they thought they could get away with. The ones who weren't angry with him about the taxes were angry with him for so obviously favoring George above all the rest of them, and they were bullying poor George whenever they had the opportunity.

Beyond his markedly diminished social life, Bradley was feeling overwhelmed by his demanding new schedule, and had grown increasingly suspicious that Lady Cordelia was trying to have him married off to a princess of Joymany. (She was: The princess in question was named Brunhilde, and was noted for being as intelligent and highly educated as she was beautiful. Lady Cordelia had told Gretsella about her plans, and Gretsella had warmly encouraged them. If there was anything that would get Bradley to abdicate, it was being menaced with the prospect of a beautiful and highly intelligent foreign princess who would probably expect Bradley to read very long books about modern philosophy and discuss what he'd learned from them over the breakfast table.)

"And," Bradley said, concluding his recitation of woe with a burst of dramatic flair, "I can't sleep at night because Peepers keeps shouting at me that I'm going to bring about the downfall of the kingdom!" He gazed at Gretsella with big, damp, pleading eyes. Bradley, Gretsella had always thought, had the eyes of an extremely handsome prize Guernsey. "What should I do, Mother?"

"Well," Gretsella said, "what would you *like* to do?"

"*Marry George and move back home and play football with the fellows every weekend and work at the hair salon*," Bradley said on a single breath.

Gretsella blinked. Then she crowed internally. Then she said, "Then you obviously ought to quit being king."

# A Digression on the Subject of a Quiet, Cozy Domestic Life

Once upon a time, the average person couldn't read or write, believed very fervently in a local god or two, and never strayed much farther away from the place they had been born than they could manage on foot before the sun started to go down. In those days, just about the greatest aspirations anyone could ever have were a full belly, someone to hold at night, and a few roly-poly babies who survived past their roly-poly babyhood. The truly ambitious might have yearned to kill a wild boar bigger than the boar that their cousin was always bragging about, or to own a necklace made of red coral beads as beautiful as the one owned by their uncle's second wife. It was impossible to wish for anything more, because you can't wish for something that you can't even imagine. Stories, when they were told, were about the gods or the exciting boar exploits of the ancestors. No one knew that they could be dissatisfied with their full bellies, loving companions, and roly-poly offspring who survived long enough to become insufferable on the subject of boars.

Then, one day, in every little village or clan roundhouse or family cave everywhere in the world, a traveling minstrel (or the local equivalent) wandered through and asked to exchange some food for a few stories. Everything went downhill from there.

As it turns out, a quiet domestic life is much more achievable than adventure, glory, and a royal crown. It's also, unfortunately, often the case that a person successfully slays the dragon, solves the riddle, and doggedly scrambles their way to the highest frozen peaks of fame, fortune, and success, then takes a moment to catch their breath, looks around a bit, and says, in a voice both astounded and despairing, "But I don't *feel* any different!"

CHAPTER 9

# Back to the Discussion Between Poor King Bradley and His Increasingly Smug Mother

"Mother!" Bradley said, as scandalized by her wickedness as ever. You'd think that he would have gotten used to it, having been raised by a witch, but he never failed to expect everyone around him to be as kind and honest and pure of heart as he was himself. "I can't just *quit being king*. Evermore would be left without a ruler! The Prophecy of Peepers would come true! And George would be so disappointed in me if I publicly abandoned my sworn duty to pursue my own selfish happiness." George was, unfortunately, just as virtuous as Bradley, despite being significantly more intelligent.

The sound of the phrase "the Prophecy of Peepers" temporarily rendered Gretsella both cross-eyed and incapable of human speech. Once she'd recovered, she said, "So we'll find a suitable replacement to overthrow you."

"To overthrow me?" Bradley repeated, his brow furrowing. "But I don't want there to be a *war.* People might get hurt."

Gretsella refrained from noting that people would certainly get hurt in a war, because that was the entire point. If no one was hurt in a war, then it was just an armed discussion. "They wouldn't *actually* overthrow you," she explained, summoning all of her available patience. "We would pick someone to replace you, and then you would *pretend* to be overthrown. That way, no one would have to be embarrassed by your abdication." Then she added helpfully, "That's what it's called when a king quits."

"Thank you," Bradley said. He was always very appreciative when people explained difficult words. "But I don't think that it's a very good idea, Mother. There's nothing in any of the prophecies about me pretending to be overthrown."

This was, if not the very *stupidest* thing that Gretsella had ever heard, certainly a contender for some sort of participation ribbon in the category. "That's a very good point, Bradley," she said. "I'll think about it. Maybe there's something else we could do to improve things."

Bradley gave her a big, affectionate hug at this, which she withstood admirably. Then she wriggled free, made her excuses, left, and immediately sent messages to Bradley's entire advisory council demanding their presence at a secret meeting without him.

"THANK YOU FOR MEETING WITH ME," SHE SAID AFTER they'd all assembled in the secret former torture room next to the cheese cellar in the basement. The flickering torchlight lent a welcome conspiratorial touch to the proceedings. "I've called you all here tonight so that we can discuss how best to overthrow the king."

Uproar ensued. Sir George leapt out of his chair and, in doing so, displayed a number of virulent mustard stains all down his front: the unfortunate result of his having accompanied Bradley to meet a foreign dignitary earlier in the day. Mr. Kedge, from what she could see of him underneath his enormous cerulean tricorn hat, looked deeply scandalized. Janet looked intrigued. Lady Cordelia and Herman busied themselves calming everyone else down, then looked back to Gretsella. Herman spoke first. "Could you explain, ma'am? Only we all thought you just said that you want to overthrow the king."

"I do," Gretsella said. "Not in a *nasty* way. For his own good. The boy needs nothing more than a good overthrowing. It will solve all of his problems almost immediately. And anyway, if we don't overthrow him, someone else will just do it for us. He's annoyed all of his knights, and half of them start getting fidgety when the government stays stable for longer than about fifteen minutes. Better to be peaceably replaced after an elaborate faux revolution cooked up by a council of your friends than to be violently overthrown in a military coup orchestrated by a junta of your enemies, that's what *I* always say."

"You always say that?" Sir George asked with uncharacteristic sarcasm. "How often does this particular scenario come up?"

"Does King Bradley *want* to be overthrown?" asked Janet, who was jotting down notes in a small notepad. "I don't see why we *shouldn't* overthrow him, if it's consensual. Does he have someone in mind for his successor?"

"I think that he *does* want to be overthrown," Gretsella said. "He just doesn't *want* to want to be overthrown."

"In other words," Sir George said, "he doesn't want to be overthrown."

"Define *want*," Gretsella said.

"We're talking in circles," Lady Cordelia said. "And wasting time. I'd planned on going over the weekly produce order this afternoon, and now my schedule has been completely disrupted. All those in favor of overthrowing the king, raise your hand."

Gretsella raised her hand. No one else did. Sir George actually *sat* on his hands, which struck Gretsella as unnecessarily dramatic. "Well, *fine*," she said. "I suppose that Bradley's poor, sweet, defenseless old mother will have to orchestrate a coup without any help from anyone."

"Oh, Gretsella," Lady Cordelia said, "don't sell yourself so short. You certainly aren't poor or defenseless."

"Or sweet," Sir George muttered.

Gretsella waited for someone to say that she wasn't old. No one did. She cleared her throat. "And *old*?"

"Younger than some," Herman said after a moment.

"Thank you, Herman," Gretsella said with more genuine appreciation than she usually felt for anyone. There was something pleasant about a man coming so close to lying for you. Then she stood. "I'll remember every bit of this conversation," she told the assembled sandbaggers. Then she swept out of the room. She magically blew out the torches as she left, just to show them all how seriously she was taking this. They'd all stub their toes and scrape their shins trying to get out of there in the dark, and it would *serve them right.*

After such a disappointing meeting, there was nothing left to do but stop by the kitchen for a nice piece of cake, chase it down with a nice glass of whiskey, and tuck herself straight into bed.

SHE WAS WOKEN AT AN HOUR OF THE MORNING THAT WAS far too late to be appropriately dark and cold and witchy but much too early for any reasonable person to want to put their shoes on. She squinted out at the space around her bed. A number of armed men squinted back, flanking her extremely unhappy-looking son. "I'm really awfully sorry, Mother," Bradley said, "but I'm having you thrown in the dungeon for a few days."

She yawned, rubbed her eyes, and then glared at him. "What in the world would you want to do *that* for, you ridiculous child?" He didn't really mean it, obviously. Her Bradley would *never* throw his mother in a dungeon.

"I've been told by a very reliable source that you've been plotting to overthrow me," Bradley said.

"*George*," Gretsella muttered. Of course it was George. "I curse you, George!"

Bradley ignored the cursing. "I can't just have my own mother running around talking about how she wants to have me overthrown and not do anything about it," he said, in a very reasonable tone of voice. "No one will be able to take me seriously."

"Is that really all you care about?" Gretsella asked. "Whether or not you're taken seriously? You'd put that above the well-being of your own *mother*?"

"I do have to take it a *little* seriously," Bradley said. "It's hard to command people to do things when your own mother thinks that you should be overthrown." This, admittedly, made perfect sense, and he said it as if he had really *thought it through*. This was absolutely terrible. No mother should have to endure anything half so dreadful as her own son developing the ability to formulate independent thoughts. "And anyway, it's only a few days in the east wing of the dungeon, the one with the nice suites with private baths. Just to show everyone that I'm not just letting you get away with anything, you know. There's no need to be *too* dramatic about it."

"I am *not* being dramatic!!!" Gretsella said, with exactly three perfectly audible exclamation points.

"Guards, please gently seize her," Bradley said.

"I curse you, Bradley!" Gretsella hissed as the guards gently carried her away.

GRETSELLA SULKED IN HER (ADMITTEDLY FAIRLY PLEASANT) dungeon suite for the rest of the day, feeling extremely wounded and aggrieved and generally put-upon. There was a very limited selection of reading material in the suite, and the sitting room was drafty. She would probably catch some sort of dangerous wasting dungeon disease and die, and Bradley would feel *very* sorry. She could, of course, easily escape from her prison, but that was beside the point. It would be a terrible waste of having been grievously wronged not to suffer very ostentatiously and make her betrayer feel as guilty as possible for his enormous and unwarranted cruelty to a helpless old lady.

At six o'clock, a servant brought her supper on a tray. The soup was too salty. Gretsella cursed the soup. Then she went to bed early and slept the sleep of the *extremely* righteous.

The next morning, Gretsella was woken up by the distant sounds of battle. This was annoying for two reasons: First, it was very early in the morning, and the noise of what she could only surmise were some man's final screams had disrupted her sleep. Second, she was in a palace, not on a battlefield, and she hadn't expected warfare on the premises. Gretsella *hated* being taken by surprise.

She considered sulking in the dungeon for a while longer, just to drive home the point that everything always went badly when she wasn't around to keep things in hand. But her curiosity (always one of her strongest traits) overwhelmed her pettiness (another of her strongest traits), so she turned herself into a mouse and went creeping through the walls to find out what, exactly, was going on.

What was going on, it seemed, was a large number of men attempting to kill one another all over the palace. They were rushing around at such swift speeds that it took her a considerable amount of time to work out that there were two obvious parties involved: the palace guards, who wore red plumes on their helmets, and the other ones, who didn't. This was somewhat alarming. Strange men fighting the palace guards suggested an attempted coup. Gretsella didn't at all approve of people trying to overthrow her son when she wasn't the mastermind behind the attempt. It struck her as very disrespectful. She didn't go into *their* houses and attempt to teach *their* sons about potion brewing or personal hygiene. It was only common courtesy not to try to parent other people's errant children, especially via violent insurrections.

She crept her way through an exhausting catacomb of nooks and crannies, got lost in a drainpipe that ran along the outside of the grand ballroom, and had to ask for directions from an astounded pigeon. Then she finally made her way to Bradley's bedchamber, where she found Bradley and Sir George, both in states of partial undress, putting up a good fight against some of the armed invaders. Sir George was wielding a sword, which Gretsella could only assume he must sleep with. Bradley was wielding nothing but his devastating right hook and, in his left hand, a chamber pot. Judging by the smell in the room, someone had used it for its intended purpose before Bradley decided to repurpose it for walloping home invaders.

Gretsella watched these goings-on for a minute or so with great interest and amusement. Then one of the strangers lunged out with his sword and managed to draw blood from Bradley's shoulder, and it stopped being even a little bit entertaining. She felt a hot flush envelop her entire little mouse body. She gave an infuriated squeak, which transformed halfway through into "absolutely enough of *that*!" as she flung herself off the top of the doorframe, metamorphosing mid-fling from tiny gray mouse into infuriated nude witch of sophisticated vintage. She had turned all of the enemy soldiers into fruit flies by the time she hit the ground. Then she stood there in the middle of the room, waiting with patience and modesty to be thanked for her incredible cleverness, skill, and general heroism.

"Mother!" Bradley said, obviously nearly entirely overcome with awe and gratitude. An enemy fruit fly hovered, fruitlessly, near his right shoulder. "Did you change your mind? And would you . . . like to borrow a bathrobe?"

This was somewhat less than the effusive thanks Gretsella had expected. She squinted at Bradley for a moment, considering refusing the offer. It was, however, chilly in the room, and it was against Gretsella's principles to ever sacrifice her personal comfort for the sake of principle. "Thank you," she said. "And a pair of slippers."

A bathrobe and slippers were provided. They were too large, so Gretsella shrank them, transforming the extra matter into some nice decorative runic embroidery around the cuffs of the bathrobe, plus some attractively witchly silver tassels on the slippers. Bradley sighed. "That was my favorite robe, Mother. I'm happy to lend you things, but I wish you would ask before you shrink them."

"You're the king," Gretsella said dismissively. "You can get new slippers whenever you like."

"An interesting thing to say!" Sir George said, swatting irritably at his fruit-flyified enemy combatants, two of which were circling his left ear. "You seem to appreciate Bradley being the king when you aren't sending armed men after him to have him killed in his own bed!"

"Stop talking about Bradley's bed," said Gretsella, who had most certainly noticed Sir George's casual use of her son's heathen name. Being near nude in her son's bedroom was one thing, but calling him *Bradley* seemed to indicate a level of familiarity that she would need to keep an eye on. She still *liked* Sir George, but she'd noticed in him an alarming tendency toward defending Bradley against all comers, including his own doting mother. "I don't like thinking about it. And I've never sent men after him in his life. I was busy dying of exposure in the dungeon when I heard the carrying-on up here and crept out to investigate."

"Oh no, did you catch a chill down there?" Bradley asked, all sweet solicitude. "I knew that we should have had you thrown into the tower instead of the dungeon. It's awfully damp in the basement."

"She wasn't actually dying of exposure, Bradley," Sir George said. "You can't be exposed in a nice underground suite. There's a four-poster down there. And anyway, I've never seen a healthier-looking woman in my life." He eyed Gretsella for a moment. "You really had nothing to do with the attack?"

"Absolutely nothing," Gretsella said firmly. "I want to *stage* a *fake* violent coup and install a new ruler so that Bradley can go home and get back to peacefully cutting hair and playing football and enjoying himself instead of having to suffer through all of this *king* nonsense. I don't want to *actually* see him violently overthrown. He can't peacefully run a hair salon if he's been killed by hired goons, can he?"

"That does sound nice," Bradley said wistfully. "Going home, and working at the salon, and playing football with the fellows. You never really appreciate the simple things in life until you have to take responsibility over the welfare of a nation and its people, do you?"

"I don't think that *is* how most people learn to appreciate the little things, Bradley," Gretsella said. "Buying horrible books full of inspirational poetry usually does the trick for anyone who doesn't have the common sense to enjoy themselves like a normal person in the first place." Gretsella was firmly opposed to Life Lessons of all kinds. There were, in her view, two proper ways to come to an understanding about the ways of the world: through native intelligence and old-fashioned common sense, as she had, or by having the ways of the world firmly explained to you by Gretsella, as she preferred for everyone else. It was much simpler for everyone that way, so long as she wasn't forced to repeat herself.

"But if you didn't send those men after Bradley," Sir George said, "then that means that someone else is *actually* trying to usurp the throne and really *does* want to see Bradley dead!"

"It almost makes you feel as if a nicely arranged announcement of your abdication, complete with a ready-made replacement, would be a lovely way to gracefully exit the political sphere, doesn't it?" Gretsella asked.

They all looked at one another.

"Mother," Bradley said, "I think that I'd like for you to overthrow me."

"Hail, King Bradley!" the toadaphone cried out from under a cushion on a nearby settee, where it had been hiding from the melee. "All hail King Bradley, Destroyer of the Kingdom!"

"Shut up, you," Gretsella told it, "or I'll turn you into a man."

CHAPTER 10

# In Which Gretsella Encounters Some Unanticipated Plot Twists

Over the next day or so, Gretsella was forced to admit that plotting to overthrow the king was much easier once she'd obtained His Majesty's consent. She had him write very polite notes to the members of his advisory council in which he alerted them to this new state of affairs and appointed his mother Chief Minister Responsible for the Collapse of Government. (The title was Gretsella's idea; Sir George had expressed skepticism about whether or not it *sent the wrong message*.) Her first task in her new role was asking Janet and Herman to nose around a little and find out who was responsible for the attempted coup. The answer came quickly: It was the horrible Sir Harold of the Rugged Jawline and his equally nasty brothers, who were all incensed over Bradley's recent adjustments to the tax code. Bradley was quietly devastated by the news. Fortunately for him, Sir George was there to provide sympathy and comfort. He also provided amusingly catty mumbled remarks about Sir Harold when Bradley was out of earshot. Gretsella patted Sir George's knee. "I never liked him either," she said, and didn't bother getting Bradley's permission before having the whole Harold clan tossed into one of the palace's damper dungeon cells.

With that out of the way, the next step was to devise a plan for gracefully extracting Bradley from power. Gretsella held another meeting, this time in the warm and well-lit council hall, with Bradley in attendance. Janet piped up the instant Gretsella declared that the meeting was in session. "What if, instead of a coup, we tried to establish a democracy?"

Everyone made utterances like "Ah!" or "*Hmm*" at that. Bradley rubbed his chin thoughtfully. No one said anything for a long moment. Finally, brave Sir George spoke for all of them. "What's a *democracy*?"

Janet explained: "It's when you allow The People to choose their own ruler every few years." She said "The People" with the audible capital letters of someone who had read a lot of books on political theory but spent very little time with the smelly and irritating members of the general public.

Gretsella frowned. "That's a *terrible* idea," she said. "The people are mostly idiots."

"So are most of the rulers we have now," Janet countered. "The People can't really do much worse than a bunch of talking animals. No offense, Your Majesty."

"None taken," Bradley said, his face gone slightly pink. "I do think that the mice and squirrels might have been a little overenthusiastic when it came to supporting my reign, because they liked the part where I was the old king's son and raised in the forest. They don't have to pay taxes, after all, so they don't have to be very practical about the government."

Everyone took a moment to digest this pronouncement. Sir George had a very soft, silly sort of look on his nice, earnest face. "That was . . . very insightful, Bradley." The *surprisingly* was present but unvoiced, because Sir George was a kind man who was also clearly, truly fond of Bradley. The fact that he was still making soppy faces at him now, when he knew that Bradley was soon to experience the world's most precipitous demotion in his plunge from king to journeyman hairdresser, made that very clear. Even Gretsella herself, if not actually moved, was at least *nudged* by George's devotion to her only child. And Bradley's insight into squirrel psychology *was* fairly impressive, by Bradley standards.

"Thank you," Bradley said, his face gone even pinker. He cleared his throat. "Anyway, couldn't we give this democracy idea a try? Maybe the people would like it."

"The *people* are very likely to like all *sorts* of things that aren't any good for them," Gretsella said, but now she was considering it. "How exactly do they determine who the people want to be their leader?"

"People who want the job *run for office*," Janet said, pronouncing the phrase as if it were the name of an expensive foreign wine. "They go around making speeches in town squares and things, and whipping the crowds up into a frenzy about how they're going to *vote the bastards out*. Then there's an *election*, and everyone gets to vote on who they'd like to be in charge, and whoever gets the most votes gets to run the country."

Everyone was staring at her, their faces full of fascination, bafflement, and abject horror. Sir George was the first to speak up. "But then, couldn't just any maniac end up running the country?"

"That could happen now," Janet said. "As long as the maniac has the right father. It isn't as if they screen princes for competence before they let them take over."

There was a beat of uncomfortable silence as everyone tried their best not to look at Bradley.

Then, to Gretsella's surprise, Herman spoke. "So, will we just go around telling people that the king's getting tired of kinging and wants to do a democracy, and maybe they might want to try their hands at the job? I don't mean to be a wet blanket, but I think if I went down to my local bar and said that, everyone would just think I'd gotten kicked in the head again."

"We'll need it to be more organized than that," Janet said. "Maybe a public education campaign to teach everyone about democracy and why they should like it."

"A *propaganda* campaign, you might call it," Gretsella said. She was looking at Janet now, thoughtful. She might still be denying that she was a witch, but Janet was very witchlike in her eagerness to ply her trade. "It's lucky for us that we have a minister of propaganda already established in the role."

"I'd be happy to take charge of the project, of course,"

Janet said demurely. "I'm sure that you're much too busy to waste your time writing silly songs about the electoral process, Grandmother."

"I certainly am," Gretsella said, forced to agree with this characterization of her importance and busyness despite her mounting suspicion that she was being *handled*. Janet was much too much like a witch to *not* be up to something. Gretsella wouldn't be surprised to learn that Janet was already making plans for negotiating a generous severance package by any means necessary. She already had enough blackmail material on everyone surrounding Bradley to power a lifetime's worth of anonymous letters with the words all cut out of magazines. It was a good thing that Gretsella knew an excellent spell for giving the senders of nasty letters a debilitating twitch whenever they ventured near a pair of scissors or a pot of glue. "You'll do your propaganda campaign, then, and we'll give this democracy thing the old coven try."

Janet threw herself wholeheartedly into the propaganda campaign, which turned out to be complicated enough of a task to require a budgetary increase for the Propaganda Department so that Janet could hire junior jesters. This was, perhaps, what Janet had been after in the first place. If there was one thing that had better staying power than a king, it was the elaborate overpaid bureaucracy surrounding him. If Janet really wanted her position to become permanent, Gretsella thought, she would hire at least three administrators who could invent forms for the jesters to fill out before, during, and after they did any jesting. However, she decided to refrain from making this suggestion to Janet directly: The girl was fully capable of coming up with fiendish schemes all on her own.

In any case, the junior jesters were apparently competent enough at their tasks for their work to have immediate and obvious effects. The streets of the capital echoed with the sound of the word *democracy*, particularly in the context of sentences such as "What the hell is a *democracy*?" and "Why are all of the damn jesters singing about nothing but *democracy* all of a sudden? What happened to a nice old-fashioned love song?" and "If I have to hear one more word about *democracy*, I'm burning this whole place to the ground, so help me I will!"

Gretsella spoke to Janet, who conceded that the junior jesters had, perhaps, been slightly overzealous in their efforts. She instructed them to be less irritating in their propagandizing. Herman suggested that a pro-democracy organization funded by the Propaganda Department could give out free grilled meat and beer on the street corners. "We could call them *community festivals*," he said. "As if they just happened on their own, natural-like, only we'll be using them to trick the people into wanting to overthrow the government."

"*Diabolical*," Gretsella said admiringly. "Make it so, Janet!"

Janet made it so. The revolutionary spirit began to bloom on the streets of the capital. A few people were even so bold as to announce themselves as candidates, though most of them were the sorts of people who liked to wear extremely eye-catching hats and talk a lot about one-time-only opportunities to start work-from-home businesses. At what Gretsella and Janet mutually decided was the most opportune time, Bradley gave a stirring speech from the palace balcony on the many advantages of democracy. Gretsella noticed the people in the crowd exchanging glances before venturing a cautious cheer or two. Eventually, some clever personage started up a chant of "Hail, King Bradley, Bringer of Democracy!," which created a bit of glance exchanging up on the balcony.

"They're sounding awfully *royalist* for a bunch of democracy fanciers," Lady Cordelia said. She was, perhaps, the biggest democracy skeptic in the whole group, though she was sensible enough to avoid emotional attachment to any particular form of government. People with strongly held faith in any particular political system, in Lady Cordelia's opinion, were to be viewed with the same gently pitying regard as a barmaid who thought that her young sailor would be coming back any day now.

"The people love their Good King Bradley," Sir George said, and gazed lovingly at Bradley.

"They love keeping their heads attached," Herman muttered. Gretsella didn't respond to this aloud—it sounded too much like skepticism about the plan that she'd been supporting—but she did take note of it. The man had a point. It was a pretty bold thing to publicly support the overthrowal of a king, even if the king in question was suspiciously encouraging of the idea.

The election was two weeks later.

The people elected Bradley with 98 percent of the vote.

The next day, Bradley's advisory council gathered to discuss the results of the election. "I sent some of the junior jesters among the people to ask them about it," Janet said.

"And the people said that they loved their Good King Bradley?" Sir George asked.

"Well, some of them," Janet said. "Most of them just picked the only name they recognized. The rest thought that the whole thing was some kind of elaborate loyalty test and that they'd have their heads chopped off for backing anyone but Bradley. The people in that bunch were pretty proud of themselves for having figured it out."

"But that would be horrible!" Bradley said.

"A clever idea," Gretsella said, impressed. "The next democratically elected king should implement it to ruthlessly root out all of his political opponents and kill them before they dare run for office. Anyway, it sounds as if the real problem is that we need to pick someone to replace Bradley. We'll just have to do it again but make the propaganda campaign about supporting whoever we've picked."

"We can't just pick someone to replace him, Grandmother," Janet said. "That's not the way democracy works."

"Of course it isn't," Gretsella said kindly. "Anyway, who will we pick?"

Everyone in attendance shifted around in their seats, not wanting to be the first to suggest a replacement for the king. Bradley sat up a bit straighter in his own chair. "Someone smart, I think," he suggested, a bit tentatively. "Who do we know who's smart?"

A few names were brought forward. All of them were noble, and all of them were awful. Gretsella waited for the tepid discussion to die down. Then she said, very firmly, "I think that we should pick Herman."

A murmur went around the table. It started out as a "Hmm?!" and then turned into a "Hmm!!" From this, Gretsella surmised that soon after the onset of murmuring, those assembled had all come to see the strength and reasonableness of her proposal. All except Herman himself, who went flying out of his chair like a spitball out of a straw and then stood near the door with the tense, coiled stance of a man prepared to make a break for it to save himself from a fate far worse than any that could befall him in the cozy, manure-scented haven of the stableyard. "Begging your pardon, ma'am, and forgive me if I speak out of turn, but *like hell you should.*"

"We all have to make sacrifices for the cause" was Gretsella's serene rejoinder. Gretsella was always fully prepared for other people to make noble sacrifices for her causes. "You're sensible, so you have to understand what a good idea it is. You already know how we've been running things, so you'll be able to carry on without any major disruptions. You have a good relationship with the palace staff because you're one of them, and with the knights because you take care of their horses. You're a man of the people, but you're a white-haired old man who could manage to look kingly if we stuck a stupid gold hat on you. You'd be perfect."

Bradley cleared his throat. "It's called a crown, Mother."

"You can call it what you like," Gretsella said. "Only an

idiot would wear a five-pound hat that gives you neck cramps and doesn't even keep the rain off your head."

"My thoughts exactly, ma'am," Herman said. "You've hit the nail on the head there, as they say. Only an idiot would want to wear the crown, which is why *I won't do it.* I'm happy with my current position, ma'am, but thanks very much all the same for considering me for the role, et cetera."

"Your modest reluctance to claim the throne is exactly why the people will praise your name for generations to come," Janet said with a look in her eye that suggested she was already coming up with at least half a dozen inspiring songs about the peace, prosperity, and exciting new tax write-offs that the people would enjoy during the long and glorious reign of Good King Herman. "All in favor of Herman running for king, say aye."

There was a chorus of ayes, the loudest of which came from Bradley, who looked genuinely delighted. "You'll make a wonderful king, Herman! You're very wise, and you *look* wise too, which is more important to making a good king. I think I would have done a much better job at it if I could have grown a mustache like yours. People really respect a nice thick mustache."

There was a long, tense moment as everyone was forced to consider whether this was a ridiculous comment made by a charming but rather simple young hairstylist with an inflated idea of the importance of personal appearance in national politics or, rather, an astute and accurate observation about the importance of personal appearance in national politics. Gretsella decided to resolve their collective cognitive dissonance by moving the discussion forward. "That's settled, then," she said, and banged her hand on the table for lack of a mallet. "Janet, we need the best propaganda campaign you can manage to make Mr. Herman into a king."

With the initial pro-democracy educational campaign behind them, the team launched their Herman-for-king campaign with the smoothness of a more than usually oily political machine. Articles were written. Sausages were grilled. Janet gave Gretsella such detailed and regular reports about the pro-Herman poems and songs that she and her assistant jesters had been spreading throughout the land that Gretsella started using them as fire starters. Herman gave a fairly well-received speech in one of the capital's larger market squares, then gently patted the flanks of several babies as if they were skittish young colts. The babies, fortunately, didn't voice any particular objections.

The days hummed along. Gretsella mostly gave occasional orders and otherwise barely did anything to contribute to the electoral cause, which was just how she liked things. It did not occur to her until a humiliatingly late stage in the game that things were running with a very *suspicious* smoothness.

The problem was Janet. Or, to be more precise, the problem *wasn't* Janet, which was precisely the problem. Janet was a *witch*, was the thing. Not in career, perhaps, but in essence. One witch knew another, and Gretsella had had Janet pegged since the day they first met. A reluctant witch, a witch in denial, but a witch all the same. And if there was one thing

Gretsella knew about witches, it was that there was nothing in the world a witch was less likely to do than wholeheartedly dedicate herself to furthering a cause from behind the scenes. Witches didn't believe in *causes*, and if they did, they would be the faces on the posters, not the modest, self-effacing personages who spent all day pasting the posters to lampposts. A witch might bake bread and deliver it to an ailing neighbor twice a week every week for a year, but she wouldn't volunteer to collect money for the Bread for Ailing Invalids Fund. A witch did things with her own hands to make sure they were done right, and she did them in person so that everyone knew whose debt they were in. A witch did *not* hold very well-organized meetings during which she reminded her junior staffers to make sure that they asked for receipts after working lunches so they could be promptly reimbursed, and that alcohol couldn't be paid for with Propaganda Department funds. Not, that is, unless the witch was doing an excellent job of diverting attention from a cunning and extremely wicked plot.

Janet was *definitely* up to something. Now Gretsella just had to figure out exactly what it was, and in Gretsella's view, there was no better way to figure out what someone was up to than by taking a few minutes to reflect, composing a list of questions, transforming oneself into a small, charmingly scruffy little dog, and then following the suspect around until they inadvertently revealed their secrets.

The first half of the day was very dull. Gretsella was forced to lie in the hallway outside Janet's office with her head on her paws, waiting for Janet to do something interesting. Nothing interesting happened for several days (in dog time, which counts differently). Then, finally, Janet emerged, and Gretsella went trotting after her on dirty little feet.

It didn't take long for Janet to notice her. That was exactly the point. Following someone so subtly that they didn't notice you was extremely difficult. Following someone so incredibly unsubtly that they noticed you, cooed in delight, tied a bow around your neck, and pranced around feeling as if they were the protagonist in a play about a scrappy little orphan was extremely easy. If you were willing to put up with being bathed, squeezed, and given some playfully ironic name, like Jaws or Bruiser, you could find out every last one of your enemy's secrets in under a week. That is, if they weren't a witch, of course. A real witch wouldn't be taken in for a moment by the old scrappy-little-dog gambit.

Janet, fortunately, was a witch in firm denial. When she saw Gretsella in her doggy disguise, there was a passing moment when a peculiar expression crossed her face. It was an expression that said, simultaneously, "Is that my employer's meddling old witch of a mother here to spy on me in disguise as a sweet little shaggy dog?" and "Of course it isn't, don't be absurd, only a paranoid loon would think of something like that." Then she gave a big, stupid smile and said, "*Hello*, boy! Come here, come here, boy! Aren't you a sweet little fellow! *Yes*, yes, you are!"

Gretsella trotted closer, allowed Janet to scratch her ears—she *refused* to admit to enjoying the sensation—and resolutely did not give Janet a thoroughly deserved bite on the ankle. *Sweet little fellow* indeed, when anyone with an ounce of sense would immediately realize that Gretsella was a bitch.

In any case, Janet was perfectly delighted to let Gretsella trot along at her heels as she went about her evening's business. Her first business was at a pub, where she gave sheet music in praise of Herman to the piano player and then sat down at the bar to order a glass of beer. All perfectly in order, Gretsella thought. The piano player started up the song, which was one of several pro-Herman songs that Janet had submitted for Gretsella's approval several weeks earlier. A general chorus of objections rippled through the room. "*This* again," a man said, to broad agreement. "I can't stand this song. Who wants this *Herman* when we've got our Good King Bradley already? Give us the good song, Janet! The one about the jester!"

"Yes," someone else called out. "Give us the jester song!"

"Oh, really," Janet said in a modest sort of way. "I don't know why you're all so wild for that silly little song. I suppose I can play it for you if you promise to vote tomorrow!" Then she offered her glass of beer to the piano player and claimed his place on the bench. She played a few introductory chords. Gretsella found herself impressed, after all, by Janet's dedication to her work. Then Janet began to sing.

*Our Herman is an honest man, on that you can rely,*
*Hardworking and dependable, a steady stand-up guy.*

*He'll keep this country on its track, he won't disrupt a thing,*
*Not like the chaos that you'd see if a jester were the king!*

It continued in that vein. If a jester were the king, Janet informed the crowd, flower sellers would wear silk gowns and dukes would serve them tea, and common manners would soon be called true propriety—which would, of course, be dreadful, hence why they ought to vote for Herman. The patrons in the pub, who had clearly heard and enjoyed the song many times before, were pounding their fists on the tables to the beat and howling happily along to the chorus. As a bit of propaganda, it was highly effective. The fact that Janet was, probably without realizing it, applying a touch of magical influence to the crowd as she sang didn't hurt. There was no doubt in Gretsella's mind that a significant percentage of the people in the room had formed, somewhere in the back recesses of their brains, the half-formed thought that it might be a clever little joke to show up to vote and write in Janet's name.

Gretsella sat down on her furry little haunches and quietly seethed, then continued to seethe as she followed Janet to several more pubs, where she watched her repeat that exact performance to increasingly rowdy and enthusiastic crowds. Janet was a sneaking, scheming, underhanded creature absolutely no better than she ought to be. Gretsella admired that. What annoyed her was that Janet had gotten away with it. The election was in the morning. If the mood Janet had created in the first pub held true in pubs across the city, then there was no chance that Gretsella's plan to get Herman elected would come to fruition. Gretsella could forgive many things—arson, embezzlement, when people spat a little when they talked, murder-for-hire—but what she could not forgive was another witch (an untrained one, at that!) underhandedly turning her own underhandedness into a scheme that benefited herself. Gretsella was not a woman who allowed her machinations to be machinated. If word got out among the other witches that Janet had twisted Gretsella's well-laid plans to serve her own ends, Gretsella might as well hang up her pointy hat for good: No one would ever take her seriously again. Janet's plan had to be disrupted. Gretsella was more than capable of that. With a few nudges, suggestions, minor spells, and veiled threats, it would be simple enough to shift the election so that the democracy enthusiasts split their votes between Janet and Herman, with the romantic traditionalist faction coming out ahead and once more choosing Bradley to be their king.

It would, of course, be awfully rough on poor Bradley if Gretsella chose to fully crush Janet's ambitions. What he wanted wasn't so very much: his familiar little village, and his hair salon, and a ball to kick around with the boys on the weekends. He had been so grateful to Gretsella for helping him too. Such a nice, honest, trusting boy, her Bradley. Such a loving and devoted son.

Gretsella shook herself, which, since she was in the shape of a dog, was a more than usually refreshing experience. She was a *witch*, by devil. A witch was *nothing* without her pride. She might as well not be a witch at all. And what was Gretsella, outside of being a witch?

On the sticky floor of the sixth pub she'd trailed Janet to that evening, Gretsella formed a new plan.

# A Digression on the Subject of Janet

The funny thing was, despite what anyone might think about her *scheming*, Janet really did care about democracy.

People liked to naysay and criticize, of course. People always did. Janet knew perfectly well that being very sneering and cynical about something new and difficult that someone else was trying was the easiest way in the world to feel very clever and superior. If the project failed, you could crow about it, and if it succeeded, you could immediately turn on your heel and claim that you'd known it was a good idea all along and had only been pointing out its flaws in order to help turn it into the great success that was its sure and obvious ultimate destiny. People like that old witch Gretsella could nitpick and criticize all they wanted from the sidelines while people like

Janet did difficult things. Janet didn't mind that at all, so long as she was *winning*.

Janet came by her democratic inclinations honestly. Her father had been a part-time carpenter and full-time drinker, as was the ancient tradition of the Findimatabar men. Their little cottage had been held together mostly through the efforts of Janet's mother and elder brothers, all of whom were relentlessly practical types too consumed by keeping their heads above water to contemplate things like the workings of the national government. Janet was a puzzle to them all. She was a voracious reader as a child, in a household without any books. Though she was a natural romantic and a sincere lover of her fellow man, her life experiences had conspired to make her into a misanthropic cynic. She was a ruthlessly ambitious young woman with no money, no connections, and barely any formal education (though people tended to assume that her career in jesting was backed up by at least one extremely expensive degree). She was a naturally socially awkward and contrarian personality who had very intentionally studied human behavior purely in order to more effectively manipulate it.

She was, to put it simply, perfectly suited to help foment a democratic revolution.

# A Sub-Digression on the Subject of Being a Good Person

A very commonly held—and perfectly understandable—idea about the nature of good and evil is that anyone who is nice and kind and pleasant to be around in their personal life must also hold views about politics, society, and their fellow man that would withstand the scrutiny of future generations, and, on the flip side, that nasty, selfish, rude individuals must be philosophically in favor of things like the divine right of kings, sacrificing doe-eyed toddlers to the sun gods, and making virulently green molded gelatin salads out of celery, canned orange segments, and mayonnaise. Janet Findimatabar was a perfect example of how quickly this assumption could fall apart. Janet was (as she would readily admit) a shrewd, scheming, manipulative person who would happily drive several knives deep into a friend's back just to use the hilts of said knives as a ladder to a higher level of fame and fortune. She was also a fervent supporter of the democratic experiment in a time and place when the vast majority of people preferred their ruler to be selected via the whimsical caprices of a lady who, given all of the available options, chose to live at the bottom of a pond.

Most people contain multitudes or, at the very least, a multitude or two. Janet's multitudes were simply slightly more multitudinous than most.

# Back to the Janet-Based Digression

Janet, as a professional entertainer, had spent a great deal of time among The People. Singing for her supper had made her extremely highly attuned to what The People wanted. She could also, considering her background, claim to be one of The People herself without feeling any need to blush or demur or obfuscate the extent of her father's real estate holdings. She therefore very quickly developed a Theory of the Top Five Things The People Actually Want from Their King. The Things were as follows:

1. For the cost of bread to be lower, or at least not dramatically higher

2. For there to be less dung of various and diverse origin (horse, dog, human, misc., etc.) in the streets

3. For knights in shining armor to have a bit less latitude when it came to lopping off the head of any peasant who mildly annoyed them (though not a *total* lack of latitude, just in case a knight was annoyed by someone who had it coming)

4. For a few extra holidays per year, especially if the government also sponsored a parade and provided everyone with one (1) pint of free beer in a special commemorative mug they could take home with them

5. To feel as if they had A Choice in the Matter

Janet thought these were, largely, perfectly reasonable things to want. More to the point, she believed in the Will of The People, so if—*when*—she was elected the new king of Evermore, she would do her determined best to make items one through four come to pass. She was passionate about democracy partially out of a pure mercenary lust for power, and partially because she truly thought The People deserved better than the watery governmental gruel that had been served to them for untold generations. The People might be, as Gretsella was prone to saying with a milk-curdling degree of scorn, mostly not particularly intelligent, pure of heart, or pleasant to gaze upon. Janet didn't care. They were still *people.* Janet was of the opinion that all people deserved to be able to afford to eat, to have relatively sanitary streets to walk on, and to not have to worry excessively about whether a knight-errant might chop their head off if they failed to tug their forelocks with sufficient obsequiousness.

Above all, Janet believed The People deserved at least *some* say in the way their own country was run. The farmers and smiths and coopers and carpenters and bakers and hairdressers of Evermore were, after all, the entire reason why the country existed in the first place. Without them, the king and his court would just be a bunch of naked, hairy, hungry people bowing at one another in a muddy pit. It was only good and right and just that the common people should have the power to *choose.*

Whether or not they could make a truly free choice when their main source of information was a devious professional propagandist wasn't of particular concern to Janet. She would bring democracy to the populace. If the transformation of Evermore into a republic incidentally happened to propel Janet to the absolute pinnacle of fame, power, and fantastic wealth, then future generations might consider that the just fruits of her heroic efforts to bring Freedom, Justice, and a New Annual Parade to the populace.

Deny it as she might, in her deepest heart of hearts, Janet was sometimes forced to admit that there might be the *teensiest* degree of inherent witchiness about her temperament.

THE POLLING STATIONS OPENED PROMPTLY AT SIX THE NEXT morning. Bradley's advisory council rose with the birds to shuffle off to various stations across the city, eager to watch The People exercise their right to vote.

The People, in their teeming throngs, stayed in bed. The novelty factor of participating in a democratic election had worn off after the first attempt. They hadn't even been paid for voting the last time, which The People, in their huddled masses, thought was absolutely typical: Trust *the government* to ask you to do all of the work of making important decisions for them and then not even pay you for it.

A few wild-eyed local eccentrics duly showed up to cast their ballots, mostly while mumbling to themselves about things like *municipal rezoning*. Gretsella felt almost comfortable around them, not because they were anything like witches—the dynamism of the average witch's disdain for local regulations could be used to power an entire broomstick manufacturing plant in an area strictly zoned for single-family housing—but because they were very much like a type of creature that a witch might summon from some dark plane to rain terror and despair upon her enemies. Woe betide any man who crossed a witch, as he might find that he ever after would have his every attempt to better his lot in life beset with forms that must be submitted to receive a permit to apply for a license, and peppered with bright-orange stop-work orders owing to his having neglected to pay for the other permit that would have allowed him to receive the form with which he could submit his semiannual license renewal fees.

Gretsella and Janet stood side by side, watching the anemic crowd of civically minded freaks trickling its way into the public library as the morning sun grappled valiantly with the capital's morning smog. Janet was frowning. "Grandmother, where do you think we went wrong? The People don't seem excited at all about participating in the democratic process."

"Of course they don't," Gretsella said. "They're *normal.* Normal people don't care about *processes*, especially not at six in the morning. They care about what they're having for breakfast. If you really want them to care about something they can't eat, you have to give them prizes for doing it." She was attempting to direct only her usual amount of nastiness toward Janet so that the girl wouldn't notice something amiss and realize Gretsella had uncovered her wicked scheme.

"Prizes?" Janet asked, as if she was taking the notion seriously. "Like what?"

"*Anything*," Gretsella said, a little annoyed that Janet wasn't taking her criticisms of both The People and the concept of democracy with the extremely ill spirit with which they had been intended. "The People are dense as flattened toads. You could hand them a cheap button and tell them it was a prize and they'd sew it onto their shirts and show it off to everyone in town."

"*Buttons*," Janet said, with clear and unnerving enthusiasm. "What a wonderful idea, Grandmother! Big, brightly colored ones, maybe, that say I PARTICIPATED IN THE DEMOCRATIC PROCESS TODAY! Everyone will want one!"

"*Nerds* might," Gretsella said with all the scornful superiority of a woman who read books about the history of cauldrons for fun. "And those would have to be some enormous buttons to fit all those words. Couldn't you come up with something snappier?"

Janet got a look on her face that reminded Gretsella of Bradley back when he was a fat, jolly baby who occasionally went cross-eyed in the course of trying to aim his own foot into his mouth. Then she shouted, "I've got it!" and darted abruptly off. Gretsella, who didn't actually give a banker's socks about witnessing the democratic process in action, decided to take this as an opportunity to stomp off in search of some breakfast. She found a nearby coffee shop, where the proprietor annoyed her by attempting to tease her about the slice of cake she'd ordered to go with her coffee. "Cake for breakfast, eh? Man trouble?"

Gretsella drew herself up and narrowed her eyes. "I trouble men," she said. "They do *not* trouble me. As for my choice to eat cake for breakfast, I notice that you sell muffins, sir. A muffin is a cake for women who apologize too often and men who lack the courage of their convictions. A muffin is a cake that feels ashamed of its own nature. I am a *witch*, sir. I fear nothing, I make no apologies, I feel no shame, and I would like whipped cream on top. *If you would be so kind, sir.*" This last sentence she pronounced as, *If you value your life, you insolent grub.*

The baker blanched like an almond. Then he served her a plate of cake covered in such a thick layer of whipped cream that it took her several minutes of determined excavation work to hit the chocolatey bedrock at the bottom.

Thus fortified, she returned to the polling place, just in case Janet had returned and done something interesting in her absence. As it turned out, she had. The polling place had been turned into a sort of workshop: Energetic young apprentice jesters were cutting the words I VOTED out of massive sheets of paper, pasting the words onto buttons, and pasting the buttons onto pins, which they then pinned, still sticky, onto the beaming local weirdos who'd shown up to vote.

Except, Gretsella realized, it wasn't just the most ghoulish and unwholesome local-ordinance-reading public-meeting attenders proudly receiving their sticky buttons. They looked, in fact, like ordinary citizens of Evermore. They were, if not upstanding, at least upsitting, or not obviously downlying. You could tell that they were ordinary and at least moderately respectable by their clothes, which were neat and clean, and by their faces, which were all beaming with delight over getting a special button of their very own to show off to all of their friends. There was actually a *line* beginning to form. This was, of course, only to be expected: If there is any motivating force in the greater universe stronger than the prospect of receiving a special button, it's realizing that other people are waiting in a long line to receive a special button too. Even the staunchest button detester might waver in the face of such a display. "Idiots!" Gretsella said scornfully. Then she started inching toward the table full of buttons. True, she hadn't actually voted. But it would probably look bad if she, in her position as Bradley's chief adviser, had *visibly* not bothered to vote. If she just snuck a button from the pile—

"Diabolical!" Gretsella said aloud, catching herself and shoving her treacherous hand into her pocket. She cast a glance toward Janet, then eyed the buttons. "You won't catch *me*, my fiendish friend," she said. Then, a few feet away from the line of voters, Gretsella pretended to pause to tie her bootlace and tossed a subtle little spell in the voters' direction.

The hours passed, and the voters carried on voting. The demand for buttons quickly outstripped the supply, and Janet was forced to conscript some ladies and young boys from the neighborhood to paste buttons together as piecework—five buttons for a penny. By late afternoon, they had to move their operations from the library to the meeting hall of the Brotherhood of the Golden Ankles, thereby disturbing several elderly men who had been peacefully engaged in sewing some bright-yellow tassels onto their ceremonial robes. Gretsella beat a hasty retreat. If anything was a certainty in life, it was that the sort of old man whose evenings regularly involved ceremonial robes *without* any tassels would immediately corner the nearest available woman and tell her stories about his college football days until even a witch as powerful as Gretsella would be forced to beg for mercy. As for men in robes *with* tassels, they simply didn't bear thinking about. Gretsella suspected that any unfortunate female who fell victim to the tassels would hear all about the tassel bearer's long and successful career in sales and marketing, a fate that, if not worse than death, was certainly worse than most other things that could happen to you while attending a beloved uncle's retirement party.

It was now almost dinnertime, and Gretsella decided to have food sent to her room before taking a nice long nap. She would take a shorter one, but she knew that the part where they had to count all the votes was coming up next, and as she didn't plan on making herself even the slightest bit useful, she thought it a good idea to be asleep when the work commenced. Not that she ever felt the need to provide excuses for her refusal to help with unpleasant tasks, but other people generally expected that some sort of excuse or apology would be forthcoming, and Gretsella would be forced to waste valuable time that could have been spent sleeping or staring blankly at her interlocutor until they got nervous and started apologizing to her instead.

When Gretsella finally woke up, it was, conveniently, just before the time that Janet had hoped to have Bradley announce the results of the election to the excited throng of citizens below his balcony. Gretsella put on her robe and slippers and shuffled down the long hall to Bradley's chambers, hoping there would be snacks set up for the vote counters that she could tuck into. Gretsella loved a good late-night snack, and she appreciated the generosity of spirit that led people to so often provide easily accessible buffet tables for hardworking employees, volunteers, and brazen witches who just happened to be wandering through at the time. Sometimes they had fruit platters.

There were no snacks this evening. There was, instead, a small gathering of Gretsella's associates, who were sitting around a table looking extremely nervous and uncomfortable.

They had, it seemed, just learned about the fruits of Gretsella's most recent efforts.

CHAPTER 10.5

# At Long Last, the Big Reveal

"What is it?" Gretsella asked. "What went wrong? Did Bradley win again?"

"No," Sir George said after a long moment. "Bradley didn't win."

"So Herman won, then," Gretsella said. "Wasn't that the plan?"

They all exchanged glances. Bradley came wandering into the room at that moment, resplendent in a new dressing gown that was even more luxurious than the one Gretsella had shrunk. "So what's the news?" he said with an incredible degree of cheerfulness. Gretsella glared at his various advisers. "Spit it out!" she said. "And where the heaven is Janet?"

"Could she be busy getting ready to give her acceptance speech?" Bradley asked. "I know she probably already has something written, but she likes to do those vocal warm-up exercises, and they're awfully embarrassing to do in front of other people."

Everyone turned to look at him. "I beg your pardon?" Sir George asked.

"If I didn't win and *Herman* didn't win, I think that Janet is the most likely candidate," Bradley said. "It just makes sense. The people know her and like her, *she* knows and understands the people, and she's been awfully enthusiastic about democracy right from the start. She's also a very ambitious woman with an interest in a leadership role; you can tell from the way she lights up when she gets handed responsibility over some terrible boring project that no one else wants to do. I wouldn't be surprised if she was running a write-in campaign the whole time she was supposed to be propagandizing about Herman. Good for her! I think she'll make a good king. She understands how things work around here, so she'll be able to hit the ground running, and she's *awfully* smart, so she'll be able to figure out the rest. Plus, she has *passion* for the job, so she'll never have to work a day in her life."

There was another long pause. This time it was full of astonishment.

"Bradley," Sir George said, "I know that you won't believe this when I say it, but *you're* awfully smart too. And you were a very good king."

The room filled with nods of agreement.

There was an unpleasant sound, like a damp thigh being peeled away from a leather seat, and Bradley's toadaphone came clambering moistly over the arm of Bradley's chair. It cleared its throat. Then it cried out, "Hail! King Bradley! Destroyer of the Kingdom! Hail! Citizen Bradley! Bringer of the Democratic Nation-State! Hail! King Janet! Winner of the Entirely Free and Fair Election in an Unprecedented Landslide That Surprised Even the New King Herself!"

"Ah!" Gretsella said. "I am *extremely* surprised by this news too."

CHAPTER 11

# In Which Happily Ever Et Cetera

Janet, when Gretsella tracked her down in Bradley's throne room, looked torn between delight at her own success and the vague unease of a young child who is just beginning to suspect that he might not actually be a faster sprinter than his father after all. "I can explain!" Janet said.

"No, you can't," Gretsella said. "Half of those votes for you were my doing. Don't think you managed to get away with something without my knowing, Janet. Your machinations were not only *anticipated* but entirely welcome. Now Herman won't have to be troubled with a kingship he never wanted, and *you* will receive exactly what you deserve."

It was, as far as a victory went, admittedly somewhat technical. It wouldn't exactly pass muster with the more discerning class of witch. If word got out that Gretsella had been forced to scramble after an untrained upstart like Janet with a little last-minute magic just to maintain the upper hand, it would be the talk of all the covens of Evermore for weeks. Not a *total* humiliation, but certainly a blow to the witchly ego. And what did Gretsella have if not her witchly ego?

*Bradley* was the answer. Not one that she would repeat before a bunch of stuffy old-fashioned witches, of course. Not a very witchy answer at all. It was more than a little embarrassing to be forced to admit that your real reason for being was something as soft and weak and dull and unimpressive as *love*.

It was also the only true answer. And the strongest witches of all, Gretsella had found—the old ones, the wise ones, the ones as dug into their power as an ancient tree into the earth—would toss aside a thousand pounds of *interesting* or *impressive* for a tiny, precious scrap of something *true*.

Janet would just have to learn that for herself, one day.

Still, Gretsella couldn't just let her think she'd gotten away with it. So she looked Janet straight in the eye and said, "*I curse you, Janet.*"

"Oh, please," Janet said. "I've heard you say that about three dozen times in the past month. You drank too much champagne the other night and then cursed a chambermaid for dusting too loudly the next morning. You never *actually* curse anyone."

Gretsella gave her head a regretful shake. "It really is a shame that you never trained as a witch, Janet," she said. "You could have been a good one. You've been denying your nature, though, so you don't understand how a real witch thinks." A dark storm cloud gathered directly over their heads. This alone would have been unnerving, considering that it was a fine, clear day. As things were, it was even more disconcerting, considering that one couldn't usually look up and see storm clouds gathering around the ceiling light fixtures. "A witch *never* allows herself to become predictable. And I curse you, Janet Findimatabar. I curse you with a curse that shall abide unto death itself."

Janet scoffed, which meant that she snorted a little air out of her nose in a skeptical and disrespectful sort of way. Gretsella had never really understood what it meant in books when they said that someone *scoffed*, and she was grateful to have been given, at long last, a live demonstration. Not grateful enough to stop cursing Janet, though. You couldn't scoff at a witch who knew what scoffing meant and expect to get away with a warning. There was another threatening roll of thunder. "I curse you, Janet Findimatabar, with *honesty*."

A bolt of lightning streaked across the room and incinerated part of a particularly elaborate fresco installed by the same historical king who'd added the cherubs to the stableyard. A prancing nymph had been deprived completely of a bunch of grapes, and a leering satyr lost the portion of his anatomy that had, presumably, fueled the leer. A few feet below these developments stood Janet, looking as if the mighty dam that defended her reservoir of self-confidence had sprung a small leak. "*Honesty*, Grandmother? What, exactly, does that mean?"

"When you have to ask what *honesty* is, Janet Findimatabar, you know that you've got problems with it," Gretsella said, with *extreme* smugness. "And from this day forward, you will only ever be able to speak the pure and honest truth, which will come in handy over the course of a career in politics. The people will praise the name of Honest King Janet for generations!"

"You're a nasty, spiteful old hag," Janet said, her evident horror mingled with what Gretsella was quite sure was grudging admiration.

"*Thank* you," Gretsella said.

"You know what a horrible curse that is for someone in my situation, don't you? It could end up getting me killed."

"I do know," Gretsella said. "And there's nothing keeping you as king other than you wanting the job. You could give it up just like Bradley did."

"I'm not *Bradley*," Janet said. "I didn't just stumble into this. I've been making my way up in the world since I first left my village when I was eighteen. I'm not giving up now just because some old witch wants me to."

Gretsella raised her eyebrows. "You've been working your way up all this time, hmm? Plotting and scheming and grasping at power. It didn't make Bradley very happy when he had it. Do you think it'll be different for you, Carrots?"

Janet went pale. "How did you—"

"A witch has her ways," Gretsella said. "Why *Carrots*? Your hair isn't red."

Janet blushed. "I got a terrible sunburn when I was eight," she said. "All over my legs."

"Ah," Gretsella said, "I see." Then she said, "Don't look at me like that, girl. Curses don't mean anything to people like us anyway."

"I'm not a *witch*," Janet said.

"Whatever you say," Gretsella said. "When you change your mind about this silly king business and decide that you want a *real* job, come and find me. Just walk into the forest and ask for the witch, and you'll be sent straight to me."

"That doesn't even—" Janet started, then gave up. Gretsella had already swept out of the room.

With the election out of the way, there wasn't much left to do but for Bradley to give a (very touching) concession speech (there was barely a dry eye under the balcony, no matter how fervently he beseeched Evermore not to cry for him). Bradley also insisted on hanging around for a few more days to assist in the peaceful transfer of power, as much as Gretsella would have preferred to let the formerly less-than-scrupulously-honest king-elect figure things out on her own.

On the day before they were due to leave, Bradley made a tour of the palace to personally thank and bid goodbye to all the employees, which set off more crying. Gretsella took the opportunity to get copies of Prune's cake recipes. The woman really did make excellent cake. Then, that evening, they were invited to attend the party that Lady Cordelia had organized as a goodbye-King-Bradley-hello-King-Janet-isn't-the-peaceful-transfer-of-power-nice-and-please-take-note-of-the-fact-that-no-one-has-literally-or-figuratively-lost-their-heads gala. It was the inaugural event of its kind, so everyone had been calling it "the inauguration," which Gretsella thought sounded like exactly what a bunch of dreary, earnest democracy enjoyers would call a party.

Gretsella was extremely irritated when the party turned out to be one for the books. Maybe she shouldn't have been surprised: Half of the guest list was made up of jesters, and they drank almost as much as journalists, who made up a good portion of the rest of the attendees. The merrymaking was at a fever pitch. Even Gretsella got into the spirit of things, drank three large glasses of punch—it was served in flames, which she found gratifyingly diabolical—and ended up leaning very heavily on the strong left arm of Herman. "You know," she told him mushily, "you're very *shenshible*—for a *man*."

"Thank you," he said. "And you're very sensible for anyone. And clever. And—beg your pardon, ma'am, and meaning you no disrespect—a very handsome woman. With piercing eyes full of intelligence and discernment, ma'am." His face had gone very pink above his excellent mustache.

"Ooh!" Gretsella said, and waggled a finger at him. "Getting very *shmart*! Getting—cheeky! Saying words with your very nice mustache!" She leaned in closer to him. "It *is* a *very good* mustache," she said.

"Thank you," he said, looking her in the eyes.

"None of *that*!" she said, and tried to spin on her heel 180 degrees. She overshot by about forty degrees, reoriented herself, and marched determinedly—if somewhat circuitously—toward the gardens for some badly needed fresh air.

Once outside, she got briefly lost in a hedge maze, and

emerged into the rose garden just in time to see Sir George gallantly going down on one knee in front of her son. Gretsella, obviously, listened in.

"I don't see *why*," Bradley was saying, wetly. "I was a terrible king, and I'm not even the king anymore. I'm just a village hairdresser, and one day I'll be old and wrinkled and have hair growing out of my nose."

"I like your nose," George said. "And I suppose that one day I'll like the hairs too."

"I just don't understand," Bradley said. "Maybe I'm just too slow."

"I see," George said. "Well—have you ever heard of a holly dragon?"

Bradley gave a damp laugh. "You've already *explained* inflation to me."

"I don't want to explain inflation," George said. "I meant that you're . . . like the holly dragon."

"I guard the door?"

"No," George said. "You're *indispensable*. Nothing else will do. And I'd pay any price if I had to. If it meant I didn't have to go without you."

"Oh," Bradley said. "So are you. You're the holly dragon who guards the door."

"What?"

"That's how you are," Bradley said. "You hold back the winter. You keep everyone warm. The cold and the dark don't get in, when there's you."

"Oh," George said, now sounding almost as damp as Bradley. "So, does that mean yes?"

"Oh, I'm so sorry—I didn't mean to keep you waiting," Bradley said. He was always, even in emotional extremis, awfully polite. "Yes."

Either or both of them may have, at this point, allowed their general dewiness to turn into the shedding of a knightly tear or two. There was also all sorts of embracing, fervent murmuring, et cetera. Gretsella, for once in her life, felt the faintest stirrings of conscience over peeping at them in such a tender moment, and tried to retreat. Instead, she walked backward into a particularly thorny hedge, shrieked, attempted to curse the hedge and all of its ancestors, misfired her curse on account of the three glasses of flaming punch, and accidentally turned the ornamental weeping cherry tree that Bradley and George were standing beside into a moose. The former cherry tree—which had spent its entire life as flora, didn't know the first thing about fauna, and wasn't enjoying anything about its new and alarming circumstances—began mournfully honking and attempting to flap the wings it didn't have.

"Mother?" Bradley called out into the darkness. "Is that you?"

"No!" Gretsella called back.

"Oh, good," Bradley said. "I thought I heard you in the hedge, cursing things." Then he took a moment to move out of moose range before he went back to kissing his fiancé.

GRETSELLA AND BRADLEY HAD PLANNED TO DEPART BRIGHT and early the next morning. This plan did not come to fruition. Gretsella woke up in a sweaty, unhappy pile of herself past noon to the sound of a knock on the door. She flailed up into a sitting position just as her son came bursting into the room, all beaming smiles, followed a moment later by a distinctly uncomfortable-looking Sir George. "Mother, we're engaged!" Bradley said.

"Ah!" Gretsella said, settling back down onto her pillows. "Another piece of surprising, but this time very agreeable, news! Please draw the curtains, Bradley."

Bradley did so, then flung himself onto the bed next to her to babble happily about what sorts of flower arrangements they might have for a summer wedding. Gretsella closed her eyes and tried to pretend that the sound of his voice was the sound of seagulls squawking over the crash of ocean waves.

"So," Sir George said when his betrothed took a second to breathe, "the news was surprising?"

"Yes," Gretsella said. "Surprising, exactly as it wouldn't be if I'd already known about it."

"If you'd been, for instance, crouching drunkenly in a nearby hedge as I proposed?"

"Exactly," Gretsella said. "I'm surprised and delighted by this news, because I didn't spend any time yesterday trying to back out of a particularly thorny hedge." Then, in an entirely uncharacteristic fit of goodwill: "And if I *had* drunkenly gotten stuck in a hedge and turned a small tree into a very confused moose last night in the middle of your romantic evening, I'm sure that it would have been a rare misstep on my part that I would take care never to repeat. If I had done such a thing, that is, which I *certainly* didn't."

Sir George stared at her for a long, appraising moment. Then he smiled and shook his head. "And if I had seen you drunkenly cursing things from the hedges last night, I'm sure that I would accept your apology."

Gretsella straightened up in bed, affronted. "Who apologized? Witches *never* apologize!"

"My apologies," said Sir George, whom she now suspected of *twinkling* at her.

Gretsella generally couldn't abide a twinkle, but she couldn't help but appreciate the conspiratorial air of this one. She suppressed a smile. Then she said, severely, "And I suppose you'll be coming back to Brigandale with us, then?" Her tone said that he most certainly would be if he knew what was good for him. Gretsella hadn't spent all that time bringing down the national government just for Bradley to end up living hours away from her in some overpriced downtown apartment. She'd destroy the economy for a second time if she had to.

"Mother," Bradley said, breaking back into the conversation and looking suddenly nervous, "George and I were thinking, ah, that we would get a house in the village, when we go home. So I'll be able to walk over to see you whenever I like. Won't that be nice?" He was anxious, obviously, about telling her that he wouldn't be moving back into the cottage with her.

"*Good*," she said loudly. "Then I'll only have to see you whenever *I* like. Who wants a *man* around the house all day and night anyway? High time you were out in a place of your own!"

Bradley looked relieved. Gretsella glared at him, then turned her head just enough to slip her clever new son-in-law-to-be a very quick wink. Before they both left, she sat up in bed. "Bradley," she said, "wait a moment. I'd like to speak to you alone."

He waited, as polite as ever, his kind, open face gone a little creased with concern. "What is it, Mother? I hope you're not upset about—"

"Don't be silly, Bradley," she said. "George is wonderful. I just wanted to—"

She struggled with herself for a moment before clambering out of bed. She was in just her nightgown. Her exposed ankles struck her as pathetic. Then, before she could talk herself out of it, she launched herself toward him to give him a squeeze.

"I'm very happy for you," she said. "And—proud." Her voice wobbled. "You were a *much* better king than you needed to be. You tried so hard, and you were kind and just and true, and when you realized you were in over your head, you asked for help, and when that was too much too, you stepped back to let someone else have a try. You were a very good king, even when you were a bad one. I love you very much, Bradley. And I'm very, very proud to be your mother."

Bradley, the soft, silly thing, cried. Gretsella, for her part, had not been soft and silly for many, many years. She'd made herself tough. She'd made herself clever.

She let herself cry that morning. She held her son and let him hold her back.

Later that afternoon, when they were prepared to depart, Gretsella held them up only slightly, having one last job left to do. The faded old dress that Janet had lent Gretsella when she first arrived in the capital was still hanging in Gretsella's wardrobe. Gretsella used a pair of nail scissors to carefully snip out the name *Carrots* from where it had been neatly embroidered, presumably by Janet's mother many years earlier. Witches have their ways, and one of their ways is to make sure that everyone assumes their ways are much more impressive than they actually are. Then she wrote a note, folded it up inside the dress, and left the little bundle outside the king's bedchamber. The note read as follows:

*Dear Carrots,*

*Once you were a little girl who thought that the world was unfair to her. Too bad. Children shouldn't be taken so seriously, especially when they have already grown up. The world doesn't need to be taught a lesson about your true inner worth. You are a WITCH. When you are a witch, it doesn't matter who you used to be or who you wish you were. You are just as you are, and your worth is exactly what it is. Don't try to argue with me. I know that I'm right, because you are just like me when I was young, and because I am always right. When you are sick of trying to prove that you aren't the sort of person who was ever called Carrots, come into the woods and ask for me. You'll be given directions.*

*Wickedly,*
*Gretsella, the Witch of Brigandale with the Reasonable Prices*

*PS: When you come, please bring some of that nice white soap that smells like gardenias and some good chocolates, which are difficult to buy in the forest.*

This errand done, Gretsella and the two young gentlemen piled into a very nice carriage—courtesy of King Janet, who was trying to butter Gretsella up in the hopes that she would undo the Curse of Honesty (Gretsella knew this was what Janet was doing because Janet had very honestly told her so when she asked)—and got on the highway toward Brigandale. They'd hardly gone fifteen minutes before they heard the sound of a horse galloping behind them.

"What new nonsense is *this*?" Gretsella asked, and stuck her head out the window to look.

The new nonsense was Herman, who reined in his horse as he drew close and immediately looked sheepish. "Uh," he said, "I was thinking, ma'am. I was thinking that I'm getting sick of living in the capital. All of those buildings everywhere—it makes the horses nervous. And I saw that Lord Brigandale was looking for a new stablemaster. I thought I could use a bit of a change of scene, ma'am."

Gretsella eyed him. He looked back at her unblushingly, until he blushed.

"Well," Gretsella said, "if we're going to be neighbors, you might as well call me Gretsella."

# An Epilogue, to Be Located at the Very End of the Narrative

So that's how it was, and that's how it went. Bradley and George found a lovely little cottage near the center of town. The village's master hairdresser decided to retire, so Bradley took over the shop, and people came from miles around to have their hair cut by the former king. As it turned out, peacefully abdicating the throne before you'd had the chance to really make a mess of the kingdom was an excellent way to ensure that The People remembered you as kind and noble, just and true, rather than as an incompetent twit who couldn't govern his way out of a bag of hair clippings.

The locals immediately took a shine to George, who they all agreed was Just Regular Folk despite suffering from a severe and incurable case of Not from Around Here. Most happily of all, because no one important ever came to the village, George's clothing abided unstained, and everyone always noticed him and waved hello. To keep himself occupied, he began advertising his services as a freelance monster hunter. In the first few years that he lived in Brigandale, he relieved three households of boggarts, removed some squirrels from chimneys after the homeowners mistook them for boggarts, and also had several genuine adventures, the details of which are outside the scope of this story.

Back in the capital, King Janet did better as king than she might have done, and worse as king than she might have hoped. Years went by. She grew less sure of things that she once would have sworn were the truth. Sometimes, late at night, she would lie awake and think, *I'm tired. I'm lonely. I don't know what I'm doing. I'm older than I thought I'd be, by now.*

One day, she would walk into the woods and not look back. One day, but not quite yet. Some witches take longer than others to come into themselves. For some witches, it takes until the very end.

Gretsella, for her part, went back to living almost exactly as she had before all of this occurred, with two major exceptions. First, and much to Bradley's dismay, she immediately remodeled his old bedroom into a studio where she could make her little arts and crafts projects for selling at local fairs, like cursed amulets and three-league boots (her budget didn't stretch to the griffin's blood it took for the full seven leagues). Second, her social calendar was slightly more crowded, owing to the addition of her regular Friday afternoon teas with Herman. Sometimes he made sandwiches, and sometimes she brought cake. Gretsella's fellow witches were all completely scandalized. All except Barb, who insisted on winking at Gretsella knowingly whenever she visited. Gretsella invited her over fairly often. Making someone your sworn enemy was one thing, but you couldn't easily cast off an acquaintance who made such a moist and tender chocolate sponge.

"I'm not going to move to a suburb and have lots of horrible children like *you*, Barb," said Gretsella, who still maintained the right to resent Barb for the right-hook debacle.

"Obviously not," Barb said, very sweetly. "You already have a gentleman friend and a grown, gainfully employed, happily married son, both of whom love you very much and live nearby in a charming rural village. And you're *much* too old to have any more children."

"I *curse* you, Barb!" Gretsella said, for want of absolutely any other retort. Then she went to plant some more hemlock and deadly nightshade in her garden, in an attempt to regain some of her witchly dignity. After this was done, she retreated to her sitting room with a cool drink and the latest issue of *Harridans' Weekly*. She was reading an article about the cultivation of carnivorous tropical plants (easy enough to do with the application of some simple weather magic in one corner of the garden—the only thing you had to worry about was confusing the earthworms) when there was a knock at the door.

Gretsella went to answer it. There was no one there. Then, at the height of her knees, there was an unpleasant sound. It was exactly like the sound of a goose clearing its throat, a sound that no one, witch or common mortal, should ever be forced to endure. She looked down. Then she said, "Oh, no."

The goose cleared its throat again. It probably would have consulted its notes if it had a pocket to keep notes in. Then it honked, "*Hail, Gretsella, the Witch of Brigandale with the Reasonable Prices! Hail, Gretsella, the Only One Who Can Save the Democratic Nation-State!*"

"Maybe later," Gretsella said. "I have a magazine to finish." Then she very firmly shut the door.

# Acknowledgments

I sincerely can't remember how I wrote this little book. Excavation of my email inbox revealed that I was sending passages of it to myself in 2020, in the initial chaos of the pandemic, and was also reshaping it in early 2023, just as I had the world's loudest and most beautiful baby. My heartfelt thanks, therefore, to the household spirit who wrote this book while I was otherwise occupied.

Thank you to my wonderful agent, Bridget Smith, who shepherded this thing through many twists and turns en route to publication, and to my brilliant editor, Jess Wade. Huge thanks as well to the amazing folks at Penguin Random House—Ariana Abad, Jessica Plummer, Christine Legon, Sammy Rice, Lindsey Tulloch, and Katie Anderson—who crafted the book into something both readable and lovely to gaze upon. Deep appreciation to the incredibly talented cover artist, Jenny Zemanek. And, as always, thanks to all of my very patient friends and family members, who helped me with childcare, listened to me babble, and put up with my giggling at my own jokes in coffee shops while I got this to the finish line. I love you all enormously.